EVEN MARSHALS HANG

When it comes to fighting outlaws, Josh Ford, Deputy United States Marshal, is hell on wheels — and this time he'll need to be. Two other lawmen have disappeared in the Moose River Mountains, and the trail leads to Stay, a small town under the heel of a brutal vigilance committee led by a killer known only as The Judge. After Ford is forced into a gunfight he doesn't want, and then sentenced to hang, the stench of death only gets stronger. They were warned. They've never seen the likes of Ford!

SAM CLANCY

EVEN MARSHALS HANG

Complete and Unabridged

LINFORD
Leicester

First published in Great Britain in 2017 by
Robert Hale
an imprint of The Crowood Press
Wiltshire

First Linford Edition
published 2020
by arrangement with
The Crowood Press
Wiltshire

A catalogue record for this book is available
from the British Library.

ISBN 978–1–4448–4588–4

Published by
Ulverscroft Limited
Anstey, Leicestershire

Set by Words & Graphics Ltd.
Anstey, Leicestershire
Printed and bound in Great Britain by
TJ Books Limited, Padstow, Cornwall

This book is printed on acid-free paper

This one is for Sam and Jacob.
And for Coop, the man who lit the
flame that ignited the passion.

1

Moose River Range

'Kill them all and make sure none escape,' the outlaw leader snarled before he pulled the flour-sack hood down over his face.

They numbered nineteen, all hardened outlaws. They sat astride sturdy mounts behind a rocky, sun-bathed outcrop. The twentieth man, their lookout, was up above them on a ridge. He had signalled the approach of the fast-moving stage escorted by six blue-clad troopers.

The trail it followed snaked along the valley floor against a backdrop of a tree-lined ridge of ponderosa and fir. Behind the ridge rose the black and grey-faced, snow-capped pinnacles of the Moose River Range.

The outlaws, dressed in trail-stained clothes and long dark coats, drew their guns and readied their mounts. With a loud 'Heyaa' they thundered out from behind the scarred rock and headed towards their unsuspecting victims.

Unseen by either group of riders, a large grey wolf sat on the top of a flat rock outcrop and watched the Concord stage as it wound its way along the trail to Beaver Creek. The stagecoach was built by Abbott and Downing out of Massachusetts at a cost of $1200 and weighed roughly two thousand pounds.

It slowed its pace as it bumped through a small stream, its thoroughbraces construction providing a cushioned ride.

Once across the shallow rivulet, and encouraged by a string of cuss words from the driver, the six-horse team lunged hard against the traces and began to pick up speed.

Buck gave his team another hard slap with the reins and they responded.

He was the stage line's veteran driver and at fifty-eight years of age, had more than thirty years experience driving

coaches. An old battered Yankee cam-
paign hat hid his shock of grey hair. He
wore wool pants, a flannel shirt, and a
trail-stained buckskin jacket over his
wiry frame.

Now, with its pace built up, the
Concord careened along the rutted
trail, and the scenery on either side
seemed to flicker as it flew past.

The heaving team reached a sharp
right turn in the trail and without a
break in their stride, took it at a
cracking pace. The stage, on the other
hand, found the bend more demanding.
Mid-corner, the fast-turning steel-
rimmed wheels lost traction with the
trail and slid out to the left. They dug
into a rut and caused the stage to lurch
wildly and almost tip.

Jack Welsh, the shotgun messenger
for this trip, grasped at the seat and
cursed. He was a slim middle-aged man
who wore a black low-crowned hat
pulled down over greying hair.

'God damn it,' Welsh cursed. 'Slow
the hell down, Buck. Before you kill us.'

The driver's answer was to holler out a loud 'Heyaa' and slap the reins harder across the rumps of the straining team.

'Damn you, Buck,' Welsh shouted again. 'I said to slow the hell down. The team ain't goin' to last until Douglas' place the way you're drivin' them. Besides, you'll more than likely kill us all before then anyways.'

Buck's concentration remained fixed on the trail ahead. He showed no sign that he'd heard what Welsh was saying let alone acknowledge the man's shouts.

'I said . . . '

'I heard you, damn it!' Buck roared above the noise of flying hoofs and steel-rimmed wheels.

'Well then?'

'Just shut up and hang on tighter, son!' he yelled. 'Cause I sure as hell ain't slowin' down. The hair on the back of my neck is standin' on end. Besides, I swear outlaws are all part hound dog. The sonuvers can smell when I'm carryin' money. And you know what's on board this trip.'

Welsh knew all too well. There was $50,000 in freshly-minted gold coins, the reason for their escort.

Buck lashed the team again and continued onward holding their pace.

Overhead stretched a clear blue, cloudless sky. Above the treetops rose large granite peaks capped with snow.

Welsh saw an elk disappear into a stand of silver-barked aspen on the eastern side of the narrow valley. High above them, a bald eagle circled ominously.

'You're a damned crazy lunatic, Buck!' the big cavalry sergeant in charge of the detail shouted.

Buck ignored him.

As the coach lurched once more, Welsh grabbed hold of the seat and looked across at Buck, who worked the team furiously, his eyes focused forward.

A loud shout from the rear got Welsh's attention and he glanced back to see that the cavalry escort had dropped off. They had drawn their weapons and begun to turn their mounts to face . . .

Welsh cast his gaze across to the base of the ridge where he noted riders starting to fan out. He did a quick tally and his blood ran cold. There were twenty of the bastards.

He turned back and shouted across to Buck, 'You were right!'

The hardened driver looked questioningly at Welsh who indicated to the line of riders.

Buck turned and looked and a string of hair-curling oaths flew from his mouth. He returned his attention to the trail ahead and slapped the reins hard across the backs of the team in an attempt to gain more pace from them.

Welsh leaned down and picked up a Winchester that was stored behind his feet. He jacked a round into the chamber and climbed from the wildly rocking seat on to the roof of the stage where he lay on his belly.

He held his breath as the two forces closed on each other and then saw the puffs of blue-grey powder smoke when they opened fire.

From his position, Welsh could just make out the reports of the six-guns and rifles over the drumming of the team's hoofs and the grind of the metal-rimmed wheels of the stage.

His stomach clenched when he saw two troopers go down in the first volley of fire from the outlaws. Their horses, now riderless, veered off to the left to avoid the oncoming horde.

The troopers inflicted casualties of their own in a brave but foolhardy act of defiance. Two of the outlaws went down, cartwheeling backwards from their horses, while a third fell heavily when his horse went down on its nose. Welsh watched as he staggered to his feet.

More shots from the outlaws and another trooper lost his life, while the sergeant's horse buckled, throwing him. The two remaining troopers immediately lost their bravado and hauled back on their reins to bring their mounts to a sliding stop. They sawed on the reins to turn them in a hurry, but it was too late. The outlaws were on top of them. Both of the troopers died in a violent barrage as the outlaws concentrated their fire upon them.

What happened next made Welsh's jaw drop. Stunned and unsteady, the sergeant dragged himself to his feet, faced the oncoming riders defiantly, raised his cavalry issue Colt and fired. The six-gun bucked in his hand and an outlaw threw up his arms and slid from the saddle.

The sergeant shifted his aim but had no time to fire as the outlaw leader, astride a big chestnut, rode him down. His skull was crushed by the horse's hoofs when they trampled over it.

Welsh closed his eyes briefly to block the image before he called back to his driver.

'The soldier boys are all gone, Buck,' he shouted above the din.

'What the hell do you want me to do about it?' Buck snapped back.

'Maybe start prayin'.'

'Hell, Jack. I'm too old to start now.'

'Yeah,' Welsh agreed. 'Me too.'

The outlaws closed the distance between themselves and the swaying coach. Welsh sighted down the barrel of the rifle and fired at one of the riders. He noticed the man flinch as the slug narrowly missed.

Welsh levered another round into the breech and loosed another shot. An outlaw toppled sideways from the saddle and Welsh smiled at his reward.

A hail of bullets from the outlaws in retaliation filled the air with flying lead.

Welsh was caught off-guard as the careening stage lurched to the left. It swung to the right and tilted enough for the steel-rimmed wheels to dig into the trail with catastrophic consequences.

The stage reached the tipping point and continued until it crashed on to its side, ejecting both Welsh and Buck violently to the hard-packed earth of the trail.

The six-up team broke loose an

instant before the carriage crashed, and now, unfettered of their weight, sped away down the trail.

Welsh heard Buck cry out a moment before his own head hit the ground and everything went black.

* * *

Somewhere in the distance, through a fog of pain and blurred vision, Welsh became aware of voices. Vague murmurings at first, jumbled sounds that made no sense. A gunshot rocked the valley, the fog quickly vanished and the voices became clearer.

'That old buzzard won't be drivin' no more stages,' Welsh heard a harsh voice say. 'Not that he would've anyways. Especially with a leg like that.'

'What about the messenger?' another voice asked. 'Is he done for?'

The crunch of sand and gravel under foot grew louder as someone approached his position, then stopped beside him. His eyes flickered open and he could make out the figure of a man standing over him.

The outline was a man he'd never seen the like of before. Through the haze, he could see that there was no face. Though as his vision started to clear, things came into focus and Welsh could see that it was a man with a hood over his head.

A shiver ran through his body when the outlaw raised a six-gun and aimed it at his head. He tried to move but couldn't. He was pinned where he lay by a great and invisible force, and no matter how hard he tried, he still couldn't move.

If Welsh had been able to raise his head from the ground and look about, he would have seen that the stage had finished on top of him, his body trapped from the chest down. The force with which it had landed had crushed everything beneath.

While he lay there and stared into the gaping muzzle of the six-gun, Welsh became aware of a gurgling deep within his chest where a shattered rib had punctured a lung. He managed a small cough and a thin trickle of blood ran from the corner of his mouth. His breathing shallowed as blood began to pool deep inside him.

He knew that he was dying, slowly but surely. He drew one last breath and the six-gun in the outlaw's hand roared and the world that Welsh knew went black.

2

Six months later

'Hey, stop!' Silas Morton, sheriff of Elk Ridge, called out to the man dressed in black who strode purposefully towards the Cattleman's Trust and Loan.

The lone figure ignored him and kept his pace across the main street.

Elk Ridge was a small cow town nestled in a broad, tree-fringed valley split in two by a wide, fast-flowing river. Its false-fronted main street was deeply rutted from the previous winter, which had dumped sheets of rain, more than enough to break a lasting drought.

'Damn it,' Morton cursed as he turned towards his deputy, Willard Banks. 'He's goin' to get hisself killed by just walkin' in there like that. Them fellers won't mess around, they'll just plug him full of holes.'

Ollie Ryder, the Elk Ridge general store owner, shook his head. 'I guess you can't tell stupid, Silas.'

In all, there were ten armed men lined up along the boardwalk waiting for the two outlaws to emerge from the bank across the way.

Morton hawked and spat on the street. 'I guess the marshal's service is goin' to be one less when this all plays out. Who the hell does this Ford think he is anyhow?'

They watched him climb the steps and cross the board-walk. Then he disappeared through the glass-panelled front door.

'That's the last we'll be seein' of him,' Morton said gruffly.

They waited expectantly for the sound of gunfire but nothing came.

★ ★ ★

'Hell, Billy, he ain't goin' to shoot. He's a marshal. He's gotta do it all proper like.'

'I ain't so sure, Jimmy. He's got an awful serious look on his face.'

'Naw, he won't. Not while I got this knife ready to cut this here woman.'

The 'woman' was Sarah-Jane Mellin, the banker's daughter. The two outlaws were Jimmy and Billy Wells and were about to find out the hard way that crime doesn't pay.

Sarah-Jane struggled in Jimmy's grip. 'Let me go, you heathen.'

'Now, girl, you just keep still,' Jimmy told her, then directed his attention to her father. 'Mr. Banker, if you please, you just keep on stuffin' money into them sacks.'

Jeff Mellin wiped sweat from his wrinkled brow and continued to place money into the sacks with trembling hands. Beside him lay one of his two tellers, Jack Bunting.

It was mid-afternoon and the dimly lit Elk Ridge Cattleman's Trust and Loan was relatively empty, except for the manager, his daughter, two tellers, the outlaws, and the newly arrived

Deputy United States Marshal Josh Ford.

Ford was a solidly built man of thirty-one and stood six-one in his socks. He was dressed all in black and his gun belt and holster were made of hand-tooled black leather. Resting in the tied-down holster was a single-action Colt .45. On the left side of his chest was pinned a nickel-plated marshal's badge.

Jimmy turned his attention back to Ford. 'Well, Marshal, are you goin' to unbuckle that there gun belt and let it drop or what?'

Ford remained still. His tanned face was impassive and his blue eyes, shaded by his black low-crowned hat, gave nothing away.

Jimmy Wells exerted a little more pressure to the knife he held at the young woman's throat. It drew a thin trickle of blood, which tracked down the exposed milky-white skin.

Sarah-Jane gasped at the sharp sensation that the knife caused when it

16

pierced her skin.

'I ain't goin' to ask again, Marshal. Now drop the damn gun belt.'

When Ford spoke his voice was soft and calm.

'I tell you what, Jimmy. You let the young lady go and I won't kill you and your brother.'

Jimmy Wells raised his eyebrows in surprise then burst out laughing. 'Damn, Marshal, you are a funny man.'

'Do I look like I'm bein' funny?'

A hint of uncertainty crept into Jimmy's eyes. Billy shuffled nervously and adjusted his grip on the sawn-off shotgun he held.

Ford continued, 'Now, I'm goin' to give you to the count of three. If you haven't let the young lady go by then, I'm goin' to shoot you then I'm goin' to shoot your brother.'

Jimmy felt dry in the mouth. This wasn't how it was meant to play out. In and out. No fuss. Real quick. He licked his lips nervously.

'One.'

Ford's shoulder dipped and the Peacemaker seemed to leap into his hand. In the blink of an eye, it was level and belched orange flame in the low light.

Magically, a neat round hole appeared in the center of Jimmy's forehead. The slug punched out the back of his skull in a crimson spray. Jimmy's limp form went down in a jumble of arms and legs.

Sarah-Jane's scream blended with the echo of the shot as Ford eared back the hammer and trained the Peacemaker on his next target.

Billy Wells had the shotgun on the move when Ford's six-gun snapped into line. Once more he squeezed the trigger and the .45 calibre slug smashed into Billy's chest and knocked him off his feet.

The outlaw's finger jerked the trigger as he went back and both barrels discharged into the bank's ceiling.

In the blink of an eye, Jimmy Wells was dead and his brother was down and about to breathe his last. Small comfort for the dead teller behind the counter.

Ford holstered the Colt and looked over at the banker's daughter. 'Are you OK, Miss?'

She clearly wasn't and all she managed to squeak was a jumble of words mixed with sobs.

Jeff Mellin rushed to his daughter's side and took her into his arms. Her knees buckled slightly and he eased her to the floor before she fell.

Mellin turned his hot gaze on Ford.

'What the hell was that, Marshal?' he snapped. 'You could have gotten her killed. I'm going to report you for this.'

Ford locked his steely gaze on Mellin. 'You do as you see fit. The feller you want to address it to is Bass Reeves. I'm sure he'll be only too pleased to hear from you.'

Morton and his deputy rushed in through the doors, guns ready.

'Looks like we're too late,' Morton observed.

Ford shook his head. 'Nope, I'd say

you were just in time.'

Morton looked at him quizzically.

Ford continued. 'You just saved the bank man here from gettin' shot.'

Ford turned around, walked out the door and pushed his way through the gathering crowd as he went.

★ ★ ★

The city of Helena was jumping when Ford arrived five days later. Every which way he looked there were people, some installing bunting, others bustling about assorted tasks, many were busy cleaning. It was the middle of the afternoon and the sun had begun its descent toward the distant mountains.

'Somethin's sure happenin',' he muttered out loud and the mean-tempered blue roan Ford rode snorted loudly. It moved its head around and tried to nip him on the leg.

'Do it and I'll put a bullet between them fine upstandin' ears of yours,' Ford warned.

The roan snorted again and turned its head away.

Ford found the livery and saw to the roan's care. He left a stern warning for the hostler to watch his back. He then took his saddlebags and Winchester '76, which could knock down a grizzly with its .45-.75 cartridge, and walked along to the Helena Hotel.

The last time he'd stayed there, the establishment had had brown carpet, patterned wallpaper, lamps on the walls, a polished counter, hand-tooled balustrades on the stairs and landing, and an officious desk clerk who had rubbed Ford the wrong way.

Not much had changed since that visit, except for the desk clerk. The man behind the counter was a younger man in his thirties. He wore a suit and string tie and his hair was slicked down to the left.

Instantly, Ford knew that he would be trouble.

'Can I help you, Sir?' the man asked politely.

'I'd like a room for one night or possibly two,' Ford told him.

Here it comes, Ford thought to himself when he received the *look* from the clerk.

'Maybe you'd be . . .'

The clerk stopped as the Winchester came up level with his nose. He paled noticeably when the hammer ratcheted back and Ford said, 'No, I wouldn't be more comfortable at the Last Chance saloon.'

The man swallowed hard. 'No, Sir, I don't think that you would after all.'

'Good, now get me a key.'

The man turned away and grabbed Ford a room key while he signed the register.

'What's goin' on in town?' Ford asked.

The clerk passed the key to Ford.

'That's the key to room six,' he said as he looked at the name the marshal had written in the book. He added, 'There's a parade to do with the Governor.'

As Ford walked away, the clerk stopped him.

'Marshal Ford?'

Ford turned and looked at him curiously. He'd never mentioned to the clerk that he was a marshal and his badge was on his shirt beneath his jacket.

'Marshal Reeves said to keep an eye out for you,' the clerk said in response to the unasked question. 'He said to let you know that he was staying here in the hotel and when you get settled, to go and see him at your earliest convenience.'

Ford snorted. 'I bet those weren't his exact words, were they?'

'Ahh . . . not quite, no.'

'OK, what room is he in?'

'Room ten.'

'Thanks.'

* * *

'It's open,' called a gruff voice from the other side of the timber door.

Ford turned the knob and pushed it open. In the centre of the small room stood United States Marshal Bass Reeves.

He was an older man, somewhere in his mid-fifties with greying hair, a salt-and-pepper moustache, and a lined face from years of exposure to the elements. He still carried himself ramrod erect.

At that moment, however, he stood there with a cocked .45 in his hand.

'You plan on shootin' me with that?' Ford asked him.

'The thought had crossed my mind,' Reeves allowed. 'Especially after that damn wire I got. Walkin' straight into a bank hold-up and then shootin' them fellers with no regard for the safety of the people involved. What the hell were you thinkin'?'

'Good to see you too, Pa,' Ford said, greeting his father as he entered and closed the door.

'Don't you damn well Pa me,' Reeves cursed. 'You ain't never called me that before so don't start now. Damn fool thing you did, Josh. *Damn* fool thing.'

Ford's father had left when Josh was still a young boy. He'd gone to fight in the war between the states and never come home. Over the years, there had been letters to his mother, which Ford had not learned about until after her death. From those letters, he'd learned enough to piece together that his father was a United States Marshal.

He'd begun to hunt him down and, somewhere along the way, instead of shooting Bass, had ended up becoming a marshal himself.

That had been around ten years earlier. Now Ford was one of the best men the service had.

There were those that queried the difference in their last names, but Ford had been his mother's name and so it was the one he used.

'I had it under control.'

Reeves glared at him then tossed the Colt on to the bed.

'Do you want a drink?

'Yeah, why not.'

Reeves poured two drinks from a half-empty bottle that sat on the small bedside table.

'Why am I here?' Ford asked. 'I was plannin' on headin' back to Bismarck when I got your wire.'

'I have another job for you,' Reeves told him.

Ford opened his mouth to protest but Reeves cut him off.

'And before I hear a sob story about you bein' due for some time off so you can spark that young lady you been makin' eyes at, I'll tell you that the job is important.'

Ford looked at his father skeptically. 'How important?'

Reeves eyed him squarely and said flatly, 'Gideon Webb.'

'What about him?' Ford asked. 'I thought you had him locked away.'

Reeves nodded. 'We do, but he needs to be transported to the Pen.'

A bemused expression came over Ford's face. 'You mean to tell me that old Hank didn't hang that son of a bitch when he had the chance? What the hell was he thinkin'?'

Reeves snorted. 'The old fool was three sheets to the wind when he passed down the sentence. He had no idea what he was doin'.'

'Can't you appeal to the governor?'

'The governor left it in the hands of the law,' Reeves informed him. 'So now I need someone to transport him to Savage River Penitentiary.'

'And I'm it?'

'Uh huh.'

'What about the rest of his gang?' Ford pointed out. 'You and I both know that three of them got away. Once word reaches them that he's to be transported, they'll be waitin'.'

'You'll be at Savage River before they even find out.'

'Why do I get the feelin' that it's just goin' to be me on this little jaunt?' Ford asked snidely.

'Because you're all I have,' Reeves said pointedly. 'Apart from Perry, that is. But I have another job for him.'

'Damn it, Bass,' Ford said shaking his head. 'I don't much like it. At all.'

'You'll be fine.'

There was a knock at the door, which swung open to reveal a tall, thin man with red hair and bright blue eyes.

'Come on in, Perry,' Reeves invited.

'If you're busy I can come back later,' Perry offered.

Reeves shook his head. 'Nope, it's fine. Josh was just leavin'.'

Ford put the empty glass on a side dresser and turned to leave. When he drew level with Perry, he asked the deputy marshal, 'Don't happen to know where I can buy a nice tombstone do you, Perry?'

Before Perry could answer Ford continued out the door.

3

Slivers of rock from the large grey-faced boulder peppered Ford's face with sharp shards that drew blood before the bullet whined off into the trees.

'Damn son of a bitch,' Ford cursed loudly as he jacked another round into the Winchester's breech. 'You'll be there before they find out, he said. You'll be fine, he said.'

Ford fired another shot at one of two remaining bush-whackers halfway up the rock-strewn slope.

'Let's see how fine you'll be, Bass, if I make it out of this and shoot you in the ass,' he snapped.

A burning sensation that emanated from his left shoulder did nothing to improve his demeanour either. The first slug from Webb's cohorts had creased him there when they'd opened fire on him. He glanced at the wound and noticed that his shirt sleeve down to his wrist was now stained red. He'd owe him a new shirt too.

'Losin' a bit of blood there, Ford,' Webb chortled loudly. 'Why don't you just let me go and we'll be on our way.'

Ford cast a sideways glance to where Gideon Webb sheltered behind a large deadfall. The outlaw held up his still manacled hands and offered them to Ford, a large smile split his face.

Another slug whined off the large rock, which caused Ford to duck reflexively.

'Just so you know,' he shouted across to Webb, 'I'll kill you before I set you free.'

The outlaw's face dropped. 'You wouldn't dare.'

'The hell I wouldn't,' Ford snarled.

More bullets hammered at the rock.

Ford had been three days on the trail with his captive and was still two days out from Savage River Pen. The three bushwhackers had jumped him shortly after dawn. The only casualty so far had been one of their own, but they'd kept him pinned in his current position ever since.

Well, not for much longer, he thought.

Before him, a slope with boulders strewn across it led uphill with a smattering of aspen and fir trees. He knew one of the shooters was around two-thirds of the way up behind a rocky outcrop. The second man was a little lower on the slope and had taken refuge behind the large round trunk of a fir tree.

Setting his face with a grim look of determination, Ford poked his head briefly from cover and drew a new hailstorm of lead. He ducked back, but instead of staying where he was he kept moving.

As he passed Webb, the outlaw boss sneered. 'Make your peace, Marshal. My boys will kill you for sure.'

With a sweep of his Winchester, Ford brought the wooden stock around and caught the smiling outlaw under the chin. There was a loud crack as teeth shattered and eyes rolled in his head.

Webb slumped to the ground still, and as he did so, Ford snapped caustically, 'Don't go anywhere.'

Ford disappeared among the trees and rocks. He began to move up the slope from cover to cover. Halfway up, he stopped behind a jagged, box-shaped rock and listened. The gunfire had ceased and an eerie silence descended over the slope. Then came the voices.

'Hey, Chick, do you see him down there?'

That would be Chick Yates, Ford guessed.

'Nope. Do you reckon we got him, Jasper?'

Jasper Boyd, thought Ford.

'I hope so,' Boyd called back. 'Why don't you go down there and take a look?'

'Me? Why don't you?' shouted Yates.

''Cause I'm a better shot than you.'

Silence followed and Ford edged around to see what was happening. He saw movement up amongst the rocks and then a flash of coloured clothing. Ford edged the Winchester up and waited.

It didn't take long for an opportunity to arise as a figure appeared and paused in a narrow opening. Just long enough for Ford to sight and squeeze the trigger. The gunshot exploded and seemed unreasonably loud in the heavy silence. The target was obscured briefly by a cloud of blue-grey gunsmoke. When it cleared, the figure was gone.

'Chick? Chick, are you all right?'

Boyd's question was met with silence and was followed by curses as he realized that his friend had been shot.

Without waiting, Ford moved again circling up and around. He wanted to get behind the remaining bush-whacker. Unknown to him, however, Boyd had started to move up the slope away from his original position.

Ford circled across the slope between rock and tree. At one point he kicked a rock loose and paused, waiting to see if his actions would draw fire.

It had turned into a life and death game of cat and mouse, except both men were hunter and prey.

Ford figured he was somewhere above Boyd and rose up to see if the outlaw was below him. He'd no sooner done that when there came the dry triple-click of a gun hammer going back from behind him.

'Mighty careless of you, Marshal,' Boyd pointed out.

Ford froze.

'Is this where you plug me in the back?' he asked with more than a hint of disgust in his voice at, as Boyd had said, his carelessness.

Boyd guffawed harshly and said, 'Hell no, I aim to look the great Deputy United States Marshal Josh Ford in the eye when I plug him. Drop the Winchester and unbuckle the gunbelt.'

Ford let the Winchester fall at his feet then worked on the belt buckle with his left hand. With his right hand, he grasped the hilt of the knife that rested in its scabbard attached horizontally to the front of the gunbelt. When the belt dropped, the razor sharp blade remained in his hand.

'All right, turn around,' Boyd ordered.

Ford looked over his shoulder to see where Boyd was. He'd get one shot and if he missed he was dead. He would probably wind up dead anyway but be damned if he'd let the outlaw shoot him down like a dog.

Boyd stood fifteen feet away, a little up-slope beside a sapling. The man looked nervous, maybe even a little excited.

'Turn around, damn it,' he snapped.

In one fluid movement, Ford turned and flung his arm out releasing the knife. It was a move he'd practised many times since he'd been given the knife by a Nez Perce chief in the Bitterroots.

The surprised outlaw managed to squeeze the trigger an instant before the wicked blade buried itself deep in his throat. The slug flew wide, but not by much and Ford's cheek felt the heat of its passing.

Boyd dropped his gun and clutched at his ruined throat. He opened his mouth to speak but a flood of red spilled out instead of words. It was a ghastly sight, but Ford didn't flinch. His profession ensured that he was exposed to death on a regular basis, and in this case, it was kill or be killed.

In one last desperate act, Boyd reached out to the man who'd brought death to him, a pleading look in his eyes. After a lurched step, Boyd fell on his face and slid a short distance down the slope.

It was past time to get Webb the rest of the way to Savage River without further problems.

*   *   *

His red hair was matted with dried blood and one eye was swollen almost shut. His face and mouth were a bloody mess, covered with fresh streaks as well

36

as much that had dried.

Another hard shove caused Perry to stumble forward on to his knees with a pained moan. With his hands tied behind his back, he was unable to prevent himself from falling further. When his face connected with the hard-packed earth of the main street, his forward motion was finally arrested.

'Get up damn you,' a harsh voice snarled as a hand grasped the back of his collar and dragged Perry roughly to his feet. The fall had added dust and grit to the sticky blood and his face was now a macabre sight.

Another shove got Perry moving again. From his good eye, he saw nervous townsfolk as they watched him paraded in front of his escort of gunmen. Every step that he took made his body scream in agony from the beating he'd received at the jail.

Perry suspected that it would be futile to think that any of the onlookers might intervene on his behalf so continued on, and every step brought him closer to his imminent death. The town was afraid. Events like this kept the fear real and constant.

Onward he shuffled, the pain causing him to grimace, past the false-fronted shops and the people who lined the boardwalk. A large tree loomed up in front of him. A ponderosa that had been allowed to remain a centrepiece for the town square. And there was the branch. A gnarled protrusion with a thick rope looped over it and a crudely fashioned noose at the end. Another reminder of who was in charge of the town.

The events of the past twenty-four hours had flown for Perry. His arrival in town, his inquiries, and being hit from behind as he'd returned to his hotel room last night. When he'd regained consciousness, he was locked away in a cramped cell in the town jail. After that, he'd been beaten mercilessly in an attempt to find out what he knew. Now they were going to hang him.

Upon arrival at the tree, the noose

was placed over his head and drawn up about his neck. The coarse hemp felt rough against his exposed skin, but he didn't fight them. To do so would be useless and only prolong his pain.

With his one good eye, Perry took a final look around before he raised his gaze to the cloudless blue sky. He was thankful for the fact that there was nobody at home waiting for him. No wife or child to mourn his passing. As he mused about his life, a thought occurred to him. One which brought half a smile of satisfaction to his lips.

One of the gunmen turned to look towards a two-storey false-fronted building with a white-washed facade. Upon the second story veranda stood a man. He leaned against the hand-carved balustrade with a finger-width cigar jammed into his mouth, grey smoke rising from its end. He nodded sharply for the other man to continue.

He turned back to Perry and asked coldly, 'You got any last words?'

Perry looked at the man with his

good eye and through puffy lips croaked, 'He'll kill you.'

The man looked puzzled. 'What?'

'They'll send him next,' Perry croaked again. 'He'll come and he'll kill you all.'

'Who?'

'Ford.'

The man hawked and spat on the ground.

'Haul him up,' he snarled. 'Let's watch the son of a bitch dance.'

4

Three weeks after the delivery of a battered and sorry Gideon Webb to Savage River Penitentiary, Josh Ford was back in Helena at the request of Bass Reeves. He was not happy as, once again, his intended ride back to Bismarck had been interrupted and he was determined to let Bass know all about it.

A meeting had been scheduled by Reeves and the governor for that afternoon but they could damn well wait. As he took another sip of his fourth red-eye, he looked into the large mirror that hung behind the bar in the Last Chance Saloon. The main door opened and a large, hulking man pushed in through.

After many years as a marshal, Ford had developed a sixth sense for trouble and a cursory glance at the man told him it was coming his way.

'Well, let it come,' he muttered. He craved something to work out his frustration on and this six-foot-four monster dressed in buckskins could serve to be just the thing.

The big man lumbered towards the bar and pushed in beside Ford and another customer. He was drunk and smelled like an empty whiskey barrel. With one large meaty hand, he slapped down hard on the bar top and shouted, 'Irv, get your damned ass up here and get me a drink!'

The tall barkeep wearing a white apron and string tie looked up from where he was serving another customer and called back, 'I'll be there in a moment, Gus.'

But Gus Tolliver was in no mood to wait.

'Hurry up, damn it,' Tolliver snarled. 'I got me a thirst that needs fixin'.'

'The man said he'd be here shortly, friend,' Ford said, not taking his eyes from the large mirror.

He continued to watch the reflection as the big man turned his shaggy head to stare at him.

'What did you say?' he asked, whiskey-soaked menace in his voice.

'I said, not only are you deaf, you're butt ugly too,' Ford announced loudly so the man could hear.

Tolliver straightened up and stepped back from the bar. The colour and shape of his face began to change as rage built within. He flexed both of his hands into fists and brought them up.

'Mister, you asked for it,' he snarled.

Without hesitation, Ford dashed the contents of his shot-glass into Tolliver's face. Momentarily blinded, the big man was forced to take a reflexive step backward and shook his head to clear his vision.

Casting the glass aside, Ford followed him and swung a hard right fist, which caught Tolliver flush on the jaw with a meaty thwack. The jarring impact reverberated through Ford's arm and into his shoulder. The effect of the punch on its target, however, was negligible. Tolliver shook his head once more, gazed dumbly at Ford, then let out an almighty bellow and charged.

For a large man, Tolliver was quick and Ford was surprised at his speed. A right shoulder cannoned into Ford's middle and propelled him backward until he crashed into an unoccupied table. Under their combined weight the table splintered and they both went down.

With Tolliver finishing on top, Ford was left vulnerable. The big man threw a punch in the close confines which smacked into Ford's mouth. A coppery taste filled Ford's mouth as blood started to flow freely. Tolliver pulled his right fist back again and Ford lashed out with a vicious chop that hit the big man in the throat.

Tolliver rolled away and staggered upright, rubbing at his bull-neck. Ford took a little longer to find his feet, still stunned from the previous blow. Tolliver moved in close and swung a left and a right; if they'd not been parried, both would have knocked Ford out.

Ford counter-attacked with blows of his own and was rewarded when he landed a solid right to Tolliver's nose. The big man reared back violently as blood coursed from his nose and ran freely down to his chin and dripped on to the sawdust-covered floor.

Moving in close, Ford ripped two solid blows to Tolliver's midsection that drew only grunts in response. The big man threw a round-house right that caught Ford a glancing blow to the side of his head which caused him to stagger.

For the first time, Ford began to doubt the sanity of his actions and thought that maybe he'd bitten off more than he could chew. The gathered crowd seemed to back his suspicions and moved back to give them more room.

Tolliver circled to his left and once Ford had his back to the hardwood counter with nowhere to retreat, he closed in again.

Ford's first blow was aimed at the big man's nose, which he blocked. The second was batted away by the advancing man who was now close enough to grab Ford by the shirt.

Beneath Tolliver's buckskin clothes were powerful muscles honed from many years of hard living on the frontier. He used his free hand to grasp Ford's belt and lifted him with ease to chest height.

This is goin' to hurt, Ford thought. And he was right. Tolliver threw him over the bar where he crashed against shelves stacked with glasses and bottles. He came to rest on the timber floor amid glass and free-flowing liquid. Pain coursed through his back and side.

With a wince, Ford placed a hand on the bar to help him regain his feet. He needn't have bothered. Once more he was roughly seized and was dragged back across the bar to the other side. He landed on the floor in a stunned heap.

A boot lashed out and kicked Ford in

the middle, which caused him to double up. He rolled on to his back and drew his knees towards his chin. He opened his eyes and saw the wild-eyed Tolliver standing over him, legs splayed.

Ford knew that if this didn't end soon, the big man would kill him. So without hesitation, he drove the heel of his right boot into the big man's groin. Tolliver stopped dead in his tracks, his face paled and his eyes bulged. A high-pitched squeak escaped his lips as he clutched at the affected area and sank to his knees.

Blowing hard, Ford rolled over and managed to climb to his feet, every breath an exquisite pain-filled movement. He wiped at his mouth with the back of his hand and it came away wet with blood. He moved closer to the wounded Tolliver who looked up at him with pain filled eyes.

'You son . . . of . . . a . . . bitch,' he managed to gasp.

'Ain't that the truth,' Ford panted. 'Hurts, huh?'

'Damn . . . you.'

Ford cocked his fist ready to belt him again when a voice snapped, 'Hold it right there, Mister.'

Ford turned and looked at the man who'd spoken. He was well built, somewhere in his thirties and pinned to his chest was a sheriff's badge.

'You two fellers have got some explainin' to do,' he said sternly, waving the shortened shotgun he held in his grip. 'Both of you had best come with me.'

*　*　*

It was the following morning before Bass finally came to the jail. Though he'd been notified the previous day about Ford's incarceration for the altercation in the Last Chance, his exact words had been, 'Leave him there.'

When he entered the back room of the jail where the cells were, Ford was lying back on a lumpy mattress atop a steel-framed bunk. When he saw Reeves he swung his legs over the side and sat up.

'Well look who finally showed up,' Ford said, his voice dripping with sarcasm.

Reeves stared hard at him. Ford could see that the man was far from happy. In fact, he'd never seen him quite as irate as he was now.

'If I didn't need you right now I'd fire your ass and leave you here, damn you,' Reeves hissed.

Ford was about to shoot back a retort, but hesitated when he saw the pent-up rage in his father's demeanour and decided, against his instincts, to remain silent.

'Nothin' to say?' Reeves snapped. 'Not like you. Consider yourself lucky you didn't.'

Ford stood and walked across to stand at the cell's iron bars. He looked into Reeves' eyes and saw something apart from the anger he vented.

'What's up, Bass?' Ford asked evenly.

'What's up is that you were meant to meet with me and the governor yesterday but instead you were drinkin' and fightin' in the damned saloon,' Reeves said angrily and turned away from the cell. He walked a few paces then turned back. 'I told you in the wire that this was important. But as usual, you show little respect for me or the badge.'

'I wonder why that is, Bass?' Ford's voice once more dripped with sarcasm.

'I don't give a damn about me, boy,' he hissed. 'But the badge is the job. It's time you started respectin' it or hand the damned thing in.'

There was a heavy silence before Ford spoke, 'You're right. I should have come to the meetin' instead of goin' to the saloon. And yes my reasons were petty. So how about you tell me what the hell is goin' on.'

'How well do you know the Moose River Range?' Reeves asked him.

'I don't, why?' Ford said.

'Because I got two missin' men up there.'

Ford frowned. 'Who?'

'Ellis and Perry,' Reeves answered. 'I want you to check it out, but if you don't know the area then . . . ' his voice trailed away.

'I do,' came a voice from the next cell.

Reeves turned his head to look at the speaker. 'What?'

'I said, I know the Moose River Range.'

'Who the hell are you?' Reeves asked impatiently.

'I'm Tolliver.'

★ ★ ★

'No!' Ford snapped as he buckled on his Peacemaker. 'There is no way in Hades it's goin' to happen.'

'Damn it, Josh,' Reeves blustered, 'he knows the area.'

'I work alone,' he said for the fifth time as he tied the rawhide thong about his thigh.

'He could help you if you let him,'

51

the sheriff said from behind his desk. 'Tolliver ain't lyin' when he says he knows them. And if you're worried about him wantin' to get back at you for that little disagreement in the Last Chance, just don't give him any whiskey. He's a good man off the drink.'

'Why thank you, Milt,' Tolliver said sarcastically. 'All compliments are graciously accepted.'

Ford turned to face Tolliver who leaned against the office's plank wall and sipped from a mug of black coffee. He turned back to Reeves and said, 'I want to know what the others were doin' in them mountains before I make a decision.'

Reeves nodded. 'All right. Around three months ago, the marshal's office received reports of people disappearing in the Moose River area. I sent Ellis to have a nose around to see what was what.'

Ellis was an old hand. He'd been a marshal for nigh on twenty years. A good man, and as tough as old boot leather.

Ford waited for Reeves to continue.

'He disappeared. Ain't no one seen hide nor hair of him.'

'So you sent Perry,' Ford surmised. 'That's what he was doin' here a while back.'

Reeves nodded. 'I sent him to see if he could find Ellis. Now he's gone too.'

Ford looked over at Tolliver. 'You say you know them mountains?'

The big man nodded.

'Tell me what you know.'

Tolliver ran a rough hand over his square jaw. 'What the marshal said is right. Word is that people have been dis-appearin' in the mountains. Mostly around the town of Stay.'

'Why?'

'Seems that they run foul of 'The Judge'.'

'Who's he?' Reeves asked.

'He heads up a vigilance committee in the town,' Tolliver explained. 'They don't have themselves a sheriff so they're the only law. I also heard that they'll hang a man for just spittin' in the street.'

Reeves gave Ford a concerned look. 'What do you think?'

'Never did cotton much to vigilance committees,' Ford explained. 'To me, they're just as bad as some of the outlaws we put away. Are you thinkin' that Ellis and Perry might have had a run in with them?'

'Maybe,' Reeves allowed. 'Or maybe not. But I want you to find out.'

'OK,' Ford nodded then turned to face Tolliver. 'Do you want in?'

'Do I get a badge?'

'Yes.'

'What about pay?'

'The marshal will pay you $200.'

'Hold on a minute,' Reeves protested.

'The man is puttin' his life on the line for the good of the service, Bass,' Ford pointed out. 'More 'n likely it'll end in shootin' and by the time we're finished, a man could get hisself killed.'

Reeves nodded. 'OK.'

'One more thing,' Tolliver informed them. 'If this works out, I want a permanent job.'

Ford smiled broadly when he saw Reeves' face pale.

'I tell you what,' Ford proposed, 'if this all works out and you do your job to the highest standard, I'll put forward a recommendation for the service to hire you. Good enough?'

Tolliver seemed happy with that. 'Good enough.'

'And you, Bass?'

'OK,' he said grudgingly.

'I know you can fight with your hands, Tolliver,' Ford said as he rubbed his still sore jaw, 'but can you kill a man with a gun if you have to?'

Tolliver nodded. 'I've been around some.'

'I take it you have a horse?'

'Uh huh.'

'Well, are you in or not?' Ford asked.

'I'm in,' Tolliver confirmed.

He gave Tolliver a wry smile and asked, 'Can you sit a saddle?'

Tolliver chuckled briefly then said, 'I'll manage.'

'Fine,' Ford acknowledged and turned his attention back to Reeves. 'We'll leave today.'

'Be careful. I don't want to lose a third man in them blasted mountains.'

'What do you want done about 'The Judge' and his vigilantes?' Ford asked.

'Look them over and shut them down,' Reeves informed him.

'And if they're responsible for Ellis and Perry disappearin'?'

Reeves' face grew rock hard, his gaze steely. 'Shut them down hard.'

5

The small town of Stay sat at the foot of a great wall of snow-capped peaks that seemed to erupt from the floor of the valley west of the broad, smooth-flowing Moose River. Fed by mountain springs, it was shallow and the water cold and clear enough to see its rocky bottom.

Behind the town, a large coniferous forest started at the base of the range and climbed up until it reached the great grey granite rock faces. In the valley grew various other species such as aspen and cottonwoods.

At the north end of the valley, the river fed into a large lake where an abundance of beaver, moose and elk could be found. Passing creatures included a small pack of grey wolves and the occasional grizzly. Higher up in the foothills were big horn sheep or pronghorn antelope.

Stay had started life as a mining camp called Gold Fever fifteen years before. Once most of the gold had played out, the town took on an abandoned air. It nearly became a ghoster but for some homesteaders and a few hard-scrabble miners that remained to provide desperately needed income.

After a while, Gold Fever began to prosper once more. The mayor of the town at that time decided that a name change was in order. He came up with a title which he hoped would encourage people to put down roots. And Stay was born.

When The Judge and his men came along, fifteen in all rode in, and just as the sign suggested, they stayed.

The sheriff at that particular point in time was a middle-aged man named Milsom. He became immediately suspicious of the bearded leader of the bunch who claimed to represent the law. Milsom's thought was that the only law he represented was the outlaw kind.

He'd never had the chance to prove his theory. Three days after they'd ridden into town, Milsom died from a knife in his back.

'The Judge' became the local law the following day. The day after that they found the man who'd murdered Milsom. A hapless drifter who conveniently happened to be in the wrong place at the wrong time. There was no trial. The vigilantes strung him up from the large tree in the centre of town, and the rope remained there still.

From that day on, the vigilantes enforced the law duties and the rope was utilized regularly. There was, however, no actual law. It was more like The Judge's rules. Anyone who broke them was hung, no excuses, no mercy.

His brand of law came at a cost. To keep the town safe from unlawful elements, The Judge charged a flat rate of ten per cent of gross profits made by each of the town's businesses. Everyone paid. Those who didn't received a warning for a first infringement and a following missed payment led to a merciless beating. Anything further and they were walked to the tree.

Now Stay was a town cowed by fear.

Almost a week after they'd left Helena, Ford and Tolliver eased their mounts off the trail and sat on a low hill at the edge of a stand of silver-barked aspen. It was around mid-afternoon and Ford held a set of field glasses to his eyes and studied the town. All seemed perfectly normal for a quiet town except for a body that hung at the end of a rope from the tall ponderosa in the centre of town.

He passed the glasses across to Tolliver and said, 'Take a look.'

The big man raised them to his eyes and studied the scene before him. He then lowered them and spat on to the ground beside his bay.

'Looks like The Judge has been havin' himself a hangin' party,' he observed. 'I wonder what the poor sod did to deserve that.'

'Who knows,' Ford said grimly. 'But

I'm goin' to have to put a stop to it. One way or the other.'

'How do you want to play this?' Tolliver asked as he adjusted his position in the saddle.

'I want you to get around the homesteads and find out what you can,' Ford explained. 'Find out about the vigilantes and the missing marshals.'

'And what are you goin' to be doin'?'

Ford took off his badge and hid it away in his saddle-bags. 'I'll be in town findin' out what I can.'

'You watch your back,' Tolliver warned. 'If my guess is right, Stay is a nest of rattlers.'

★ ★ ★

The roan protested and flared his nostrils at the stench of the bloated body that barely swayed in the breeze. Ford guessed he'd been dead for a couple of days, maybe three. The face had changed colour and the clothing was stained with the body's excretions.

61

His nose wrinkled at the offensive odour and he sympathized with the horse's protests. Ford shook his head in disgust.

'Have a problem, Stranger?' a gravelly voice commented from behind Ford.

He turned the roan so that he faced the speaker and saw three men standing there. All wore dark pants and long black duster coats. Low-crowned hats covered their bearded faces and their hands held Winchesters. The bulges at their sides told Ford that they had six-guns hidden under the coats.

Ford let his gaze linger for a drawn-out moment before responding.

'No problem,' he told them. 'I just don't see the sense in leavin' a body hangin' around so long that it starts to stink up the place is all. Bein' such a pretty lookin' place with nice people and all.'

The man in the centre eyed him coldly. 'Are you makin' fun of us, Stranger?'

Ford just shrugged.

The man continued, 'We don't much like smart-mouthed strangers about here. What's your name? I didn't catch it.'

'I didn't give it.'

'He's a smart one, ain't he, Jesse?' commented the man on the left.

The man named Jesse nodded. 'What is it that brings you to Stay?'

'Supplies and a bed,' Ford answered.

'And then you'll be movin' on,' Jesse said.

'I ain't decided yet.'

Jesse shook his head. 'Nope, you'll be movin' on or you'll go before The Judge.'

Ford feigned innocence. 'What for? I ain't done nothin' wrong.'

The man on the right sniggered. 'Trust me friend, when Jesse says you'll be gone, you'll be gone. Or me and Jesse and Talbot here will come lookin' for you and help you along.'

Without another word the three men turned and walked away. Ford watched them go and saw them step on to the boardwalk and disappear inside a twin storey white-washed building. Like most of the others along the street, it was false-fronted. He glanced up at the second storey and saw a man standing there smoking a cigar. Like the other three, he had a beard and wore a long black coat.

Ford likened him to a monarch watching over his subjects and decided at that moment that this man was the one they called The Judge.

Ford guided the roan farther along the street until he found the livery. He found the hostler, a short man named Cleve Foster, to be a rather talkative man up to the point that he asked about the men in black.

'Who are the fellers I saw with the dark coats on?' he asked Foster.

'The law,' he said.

'I didn't see no badges.'

'You won't neither. How long are you stayin'?'

'Maybe a couple of days,' Ford told him.

'You might want to stay clear of them

64

fellers then,' Foster advised.

'Why's that?'

Foster remained silent and began to turn away.

'Watch out for the roan,' Ford warned. 'He's a mean one.'

'I'll remember that.'

'Do you remember a couple of fellers who went by the names of Ellis and Perry coming to town?' Ford pressed.

'Your best place to find a room is the Aspen Hotel,' Foster offered, as he ignored the question. 'You probably rode past it on the way in.'

Foster walked off, past the stalls towards the back of the stables and out through the double rear doors.

After he'd gone, Ford took his saddlebags and hid them in the roan's stall where he figured they'd be safe until he was ready to ride out.

*　*　*

The Aspen Hotel was a small double-storey building with a tiny reception

65

area and a narrow staircase that ran up to a first-floor landing. The front door was made of a solid timber, possibly cedar, and the reception area floor was worn floorboards. In the centre of the space was an old trodden-down mat.

Ford crossed to the battered counter and rang the slightly rusted bell. He waited for half a minute before a well-dressed man with grey hair appeared at the top of the stairs and carefully made his way down.

As he approached the counter he looked at Ford and asked, 'How long?'

'What?'

'I take it you're here for a room,' he pointed out. 'How long do you want it for?'

Ford nodded. 'One, maybe two nights.'

'It'll cost you two dollars a night,' the clerk informed him.

While Ford dug out some money, the clerk turned away to get a room key. When he turned back to give Ford the key, he noticed two five dollar notes sitting on the counter.

'Um, that is way too much, Sir.'

'Maybe,' Ford allowed, 'but I was hopin' it might buy me a little information.'

The man looked at him hesitantly. 'What information?'

'I'm lookin' for two men,' Ford explained. 'Could be they came through here. Their names were Ellis and Perry.'

Ford noticed the flicker of recognition in the clerk's eyes. It was almost imperceptible, but it was there.

The clerk shook his head. 'No Sir, I don't believe I ever heard of them.'

'Maybe I could have a quick look through your register and see if their names are there,' Ford said as he grabbed the book and began to flip through the pages.

The clerk made to snatch it back, but Ford drew away until it was out of reach. He ran a finger down each page until it stopped on one name. Chuck Ellis.

'I thought you said that the fellers

I'm lookin' for haven't been here?' Ford demanded. 'Yet here I find one of the names I inquired about.'

There was movement at the top of the stairs and the desk clerk looked up. Alarm spread across his face and Ford turned to look for himself. Staring back was another bearded man dressed in a long black coat.

'Give the man his room key, Alistair, and get him his change,' the man drawled.

The clerk shoved the key into Ford's hand and gave him the required change. There was a look of raw fear in the man's eyes, as though he thought he was about to die.

'It . . . the room . . . ' he stammered.

'I'm sure I can find it,' Ford said and thanked him.

He climbed the stairs to the landing and once he drew level, the bearded man said quietly, 'It don't pay for strangers to ask too many questions. People like to keep to themselves otherwise some might take offence.'

Ford paused and stared at the man. 'Are you one of them?'

The man shrugged. 'Could be.'

'I'll remember that.'

'You do that.'

* ★ *

Ford found the room to his liking. It may have been small but was relatively clean and the window looked out across the street. He dropped the rifle and the saddlebags on a soft-looking bed and crossed to the window.

Down below he saw the bearded man from the top of the stairs cross the street and head into the Cedar Log Saloon. Within a minute, he emerged with two others, one of which took up a seat on the boardwalk and proceeded to keep vigil on the hotel.

Everything told him that he was in the right place, that the answers to all of his questions were here in Stay. *If* he didn't disappear like the others.

But first, he wanted something to eat.

6

Mordecai Wakefield sat on a blood-coloured lounge with his white shirt open. Exposed was a well-muscled torso complete with bullet scars and a thick mat of hair. On either side of him was a whore dressed only in a corset. One nuzzled his neck beneath his thick beard while the other ran her fingers through his dark hair.

The stub of a cigar was jammed between his lips while he stared disinterestedly into a large mirror that hung horizontally on the far wall. The room was large and had carpet on the floor. The bed was oversized, as was the hardwood dresser against the wall. The luxuriousness of the room was over-shadowed by a large set of twin glass-panelled doors that opened out on to the second-floor balcony.

The two girls were from The Pink

Palace, an establishment which Wakefield had inserted himself into as partner to Hilary Best, the lady who ran it. That way he was able to share in the profits and the girls. At that particular moment, he had other things on his mind. His thoughts were focused entirely on the stranger who'd ridden into town.

There was a knock on the dark-timber door and Wakefield snapped from his trance and called out, 'Yeah, who is it?'

'It's Gil,' a voice came through the door. 'I need to talk to you, Judge.'

'The door's open,' Wakefield told him.

Gil opened the door but at the sight of the two whores said, 'You want I should come back?'

'Nope, they're just leavin',' Wakefield explained.

The whore nuzzling his neck pulled back with a confused expression on her face. 'We were?'

'Yeah, you were,' Wakefield confirmed. 'Now get the hell out.'

71

They both began to protest but were cut short.

'Get out!' Wakefield roared.

They both pouted at him but dressed quickly and left.

'What is it you want?' Wakefield asked.

'There's a new feller in town,' he informed his boss, 'and I think he could be trouble.'

'Is he a feller dressed in black clothes?'

Gill nodded.

'Jesse checked him out not long ago,' Wakefield explained. 'He said he was just a drifter passin' through.'

'I ain't so sure,' Gil said doubtfully. 'I just came from The Aspen and he was askin' the clerk there some questions.'

Wakefield leaned forward on the lounge. 'What questions?'

'About them two marshals that came here,' Gil told him. 'If I hadn't of been there the damned fool would have told him everythin'. I got Luther watchin' him from across the street and I sent

Zeb along to the livery to find out what he can from Foster.'

'Do you think he's law?' asked Wakefield, then snorted at the question. 'Who am I kiddin'? Of course, he's damned law.'

'Do you think he's the feller that the last federal man told Jesse they'd send?' Gill proposed. 'What was his name?'

'Ford,' Wakefield informed him.

'That's it. Do you think it could be him?'

'I guess there's one way to find out,' Wakefield answered. 'Get Jesse and Luther and round him up. Bring him here to me so I can talk to him.'

'Sure, I'll go do it right now.'

Gil hurried out and left Wakefield sitting on the lounge to ponder the situation. The last thing he wanted was to kill another federal marshal. But if it was necessary to keep their secret then he would.

* * *

A plate of steaming food was placed in front of Ford by a young woman with long black hair who smiled warmly. Her gaze shifted to the table beside the door where a man, dressed in his black coat sat, and her smile faded quickly.

'Don't worry none about him, Miss,' Ford tried to reassure her, 'he's here for me.'

She smiled wanly and said to him, 'Enjoy your meal.'

He picked up his knife and fork. 'I sure do intend to.'

He watched her go as she headed back to the kitchen.

The café was long and narrow with two rows of tables. They ran the length of each side wall and left a central aisle. The tables were covered with table-cloths and sparsely populated with diners. Ford looked at his meal of beef, potatoes, and gravy and just knew it was going to taste good.

The seat he had chosen to sit at gave him full view of the front door of the diner so Ford saw the two black-coated men enter. The man who had spoken to Ford at the hotel was one of them. He placed the knife on to his plate and dropped his right hand below the table and drew the Peacemaker as a precaution and left it on his lap.

The pair stopped at the table that their friend sat at and spoke briefly before all three approached Ford's table where he was using his fork to eat his potato.

When they stopped, Ford ignored them and kept eating. There was a heavy silence before one of them said, 'Meal's over, Stranger. The Judge wants to see you.'

Ford kept eating.

'Didn't you hear Jesse?' another of the trio snapped. 'He said The Judge wants to see you.'

Ford finally looked up from his meal and stared at the three men with their bearded faces.

'The Judge will have to wait until I've finished my meal,' Ford said casually as he looked the one called Jesse in the eye. He remembered him from his first encounter as he took in the lynching victim.

Jesse swept back the right side of his long coat and dropped his hand to the butt of a .45 calibre Colt.

'The Judge don't wait,' he told Ford coldly.

From beneath the table came the dry triple-click of the Peacemaker's hammer going back. 'Like I said, he'll have to wait.'

All eyes in the room turned towards the men.

'There's three of us,' Jesse pointed out.

'I can count,' Ford said as he shovelled another forkful of potato into his mouth.

'Do you really want to go up against us?' Jesse asked him.

'Especially when we have you out-gunned?'

Ford lay his fork down beside his plate and waited until he swallowed before he spoke.

'Now, I know you might be dumb or even a little ignorant,' Ford said in an insulting tone, 'but I sure as hell don't think you're deaf. You and I both know that I got me a six-killer all cocked and pointed at your belly beneath this here table. So if you want to make your play here and now, then have at it or let me finish my meal in peace.'

Jesse's face turned red beneath his beard and his voice took on a slight tremor as he turned to speak to Gil. 'Go and tell The Judge we'll be along directly.'

'But . . .'

'Just do it, damn you,' Jesse snarled.

Ford watched as Gil left then turned his gaze back to Jesse. 'Are you two goin' to just stand there and watch me eat or what?'

Both men walked over to a vacant table and sat. Ford took his time as he ate, savouring every mouthful. He had to admit that it was one of the best meals he'd had in a long time.

Once his plate was empty, he left

some money on the table and stood up. His shadows did the same. As he walked towards the door they stepped in front of him to block his path. Ford smiled at them mirthlessly and said, 'Let's go and see your boss.'

★ ★ ★

'It's about damn time you got here,' Wakefield snapped and glared at the men as they entered.

'Couldn't be helped, Judge,' Jesse informed him.

Wakefield let his hot gaze linger on his man then turned his flinty grey eyes on Ford.

'Who are you?' he demanded.

Ford studied the man on the lounge before him. He had a beard like the others, the skin that was visible was lined and Ford guessed he was around six-one tall. He was solidly built and the facial hair made his age hard to pick, but he guessed the man was somewhere in his late thirties. There seemed to be something very familiar about the man that Ford thought he recognized.

'Who are you?' Ford asked in response.

'You can call me Judge,' Wakefield said curtly. 'I maintain law and order around here. Now who are you?'

'Vigilante Law?'

'My law!' Wakefield roared.

'Are all you fellers brothers or somethin'?' Ford asked him casually. 'Or is it that you all like the same clothes and facial hairstyles?'

There was movement to Ford's left from Jesse, but a glowering look from Wakefield stopped him.

'I'll ask you again. What is your name?'

'Josh.'

'Josh who?'

'Just Josh.'

Wakefield's mouth clamped to a thin line. 'Well, just Josh, what brings you to Stay?'

Ford shrugged as he glanced around the room. 'Passin' through.'

'Why would a man who's passin' through be askin' about two federal marshals?'

Ford paused briefly and said, 'Nice room you have here. Ain't seen one like it since I was in Dodge six years back.'

Wakefield said nothing, but Ford saw the slight flicker in the man's eyes.

'Were they here?' Ford asked.

'Who?'

'The fellers I'm lookin' for.'

'They were,' Wakefield confirmed.

'What happened to them?' Ford inquired.

'They left.'

'Where'd they go?'

'I've no idea,' Wakefield said. 'I don't even know why they came here in the first place. I didn't send for them. Like I said, we take care of the law.'

'You won't mind if I ask a few more questions around town then?' Ford commented. 'Maybe someone might know.'

Wakefield's face became hard like granite. 'You leave the townsfolk alone.

They don't need you harassing them for an answer I've already given you.'

The door to the room opened and another man entered. In his left hand, he carried saddlebags. The object that he carried in his right hand interested Ford more.

The man approached the Judge and handed him something. Ford could only guess what it was, but knew that he was right.

Wakefield took the object then held it up. Just as Ford suspected, it was his badge.

He smiled coldly. 'Hmmm, how about we start again, *Marshal*.'

7

'I'll be havin' that badge back if you don't mind,' Ford said as he held out his hand.

Wakefield stared at Ford then down at the nickel-plated badge in his own hard brown hand before he tossed it across to him.

'I'm waiting to find out why you are in my town, Marshal,' Wakefield said.

'You know why,' Ford explained as he pinned the badge to his shirt. 'I'm lookin' for two marshals. You told me they have left, but you don't know where they went. So tomorrow I shall continue my search.'

'I'm sorry we could be of no assistance to you,' Wakefield apologized then suggested, 'You might try Potter's Field. It's about a day and a half north of here. They could have gone there. In the meantime, if they show up here I'll let them know you're lookin' for them.'

Ford nodded, 'I'd sure appreciate it if you could.'

A large smile split Wakefield's face. 'It would be my pleasure.'

Wakefield watched Ford cautiously as he collected his saddlebags and left.

'I don't like it,' Jesse commented.

'Neither do I,' agreed Wakefield. 'Let the others know to keep an eye on him and inform me of what he does.'

Jesse couldn't help but notice the worried expression on his face.

'What's up?' he asked.

'I have a feelin' that he knows me.'

'How?'

'The reference he made to Dodge,' Wakefield explained.

Jesse was puzzled. 'So?'

'I was arrested in Dodge six years ago by a marshal named Reeves,' Wakefield continued. 'He had a young feller with him. His son, in fact, though you wouldn't know it the way they spoke to each other.'

'And you think that's him?' Jesse pressed.

'I do. Gentlemen, you have just met United States Deputy Marshal, Josh Ford.'

* * *

Ford walked towards the hotel along a sparsely lit boardwalk. The cool mountain air was clean and refreshing against his exposed skin but he barely noticed it. His mind was focused elsewhere.

What the hell was Mordecai Wakefield doin' in Stay? he thought to himself. The last time he'd come across him was in Dodge. Bass had arrested him for a stage robbery and the last he'd heard was that Wakefield had been sent to the Pen for ten years. That was six years ago.

Ford shrugged. It didn't matter. His first job was to find out what happened to Ellis and Perry. Wakefield was secondary. Although deep down he knew that Wakefield was behind it all.

Ford entered the hotel and was greeted by the desk clerk. 'Is everything to your satisfaction Mr ahh . . . ?'

'Just call me Ford, Marshal Ford.'

The clerk's face paled significantly in the lamplight.

'I was just visitin' with The Judge and he was tellin' me that the two men I am lookin' for were here but they left,' Ford explained.

The clerk nodded hesitantly. 'Ahh, yes that's right. I remember now, both men only spent one night here before they left.'

'You don't happen to know where they went, do you?'

Again the hesitation. 'Ahh, no. Definitely not. No sir.'

The fear in the man's eyes told Ford not to push any harder, so he decided that he'd try again tomorrow. He said goodnight to the clerk and climbed the stairs to his room.

Once inside, he lit the lamp on the nightstand and placed a chair under the doorknob. He removed his boots and gun belt and shoved the Peacemaker beneath his pillow.

He then lay back on the bed and everything began to run through his mind.

★ ★ ★

Two hours later a shadow moved stealthily in the darkened hallway. It stopped outside Ford's room and hesitated briefly before it bent down. The figure slid a folded piece of paper under his door and was about to rise when the dry triple-click of a gun hammer going back sounded unbelievably loud in the hall.

The person froze as a cold gun barrel pressed into the exposed skin of the neck.

'Get up, nice and slow,' the man with the gun ordered.

The person started to speak but was cut off when the man hissed, 'Shut up!'

'Is there anybody out there?' came a muffled voice from within the room.

The gunman leaned in close and snarled softly, 'Start walkin' or I'll put a slug in you.'

On trembling legs, the person moved forward along the hall. There was no sign of anyone when Ford opened the door, a cocked six-gun in his fist. He looked both ways down the empty hallway, raised his eyebrows and shook his head. He then stepped back into his room and closed the door.

There was a rustle at his feet and Ford looked down. Laying on the worn carpet was a folded piece of paper. He bent down, picked it up and crossed the room and lit the lamp. He saw that there was writing on it. It said: They didn't leave!

Ford read it once more and decided that it only meant one thing. Ellis and Perry had never left Stay. That left only two distinct possibilities. They were being held captive or they were dead and buried.

Either way, he was determined to find out and he was pretty certain he knew who had left the note but he'd see to that tomorrow. For now, he just wanted sleep.

★ ★ ★

'What do you want done with him?' Jesse asked and pointed to the crumpled heap that lay unmoving in the empty stall.

Dull lantern light lit the inside of the livery stable, casting an orange glow about the interior, which was broken up by the long shadows of the four men.

'Hang him,' Wakefield grunted.

'Are you sure?' Jesse asked, a hint of concern in his voice. 'What about Ford?'

'I don't give a damn about Ford,' Wakefield spat caustically. 'This is my town, not his. The people of Stay need to understand that if they talk out of turn, there will be consequences. If Ford wants to cause trouble, then we'll get rid of him. In case you haven't noticed, in this town, even marshals hang.'

Jesse thought for a brief moment, hesitated then said, 'Mordecai, why don't we split the loot and get out of town while the gettin's good? I think the situation is goin' to reach a point real soon and then it's goin' to spiral out of control.'

Wakefield glared at his segundo. 'We'll go when I say so and not before. Just remember, I run this outfit, not you. Is that clear?'

'Hell, Mordecai . . . '

'Don't call me Mordecai. Is that clear, Jesse?'

'Yeah,' Jesse nodded.

'Good, I'm glad we got that sorted,' Wakefield said. He then stabbed a rough finger at the man in the stall. 'Now go and string that blabber-mouthed son of a bitch up.'

* * *

Ford was up early the following morning, keen to track down the person responsible for the previous

89

night's note. He dressed and made his way downstairs. He walked up to the counter and rang the bell. To his surprise a different clerk appeared from the office.

'Can I help you?' the clerk asked.

Ford frowned at the tall, thin man in front of him.

'Where's the other guy?' he asked.

'What . . . what other guy, Sir?'

Ford could see the man was instantly afraid. It was as plain as the nose on his face. 'The feller who was on the desk yesterday and again last night.'

'He's not here.'

'I can see that. Now tell me where I might find him, it's important.'

'I . . . I don't know,' the man said in a pleading voice.

Ford opened the left side of his jacket revealing his badge. The new clerk's eyes bulged and his face fell.

'Where is he?' Ford asked again.

'The tree,' he answered Ford, refusing to meet his gaze. 'He's at the hanging tree.'

It took a moment for Ford to digest what he was being told. When the penny dropped, he hurried out the door and on to the boardwalk.

He cast his gaze along the street to where the giant tree stood, a golden hue on one side from the early morning sun. Beneath its largest branch hung a man's body. Not the same putrefied corpse as the day before. This body had on different clothes.

Ford flipped off the rawhide thong from the Peacemaker's hammer and stepped out into the street. He walked steadily towards the tree. As he approached, he noted the black-coated men who stood spaced out on the boardwalks either side of the street.

He let his hand rest on the butt of the six-gun while he kept moving. There were eight of them. Eight vigilantes making sure he was aware of their presence. It was an open act of defiance from Wakefield. The hell of it was, Ford would be able to do nothing. He was way outnumbered and the son of a bitch Wakefield knew it.

When Ford reached the body, he walked around the front of it and looked up at the purplish face. He noted the marks that indicated that the man had been severely beaten before his death. It was the body of the clerk as he'd expected, which confirmed Ford's suspicion that he'd been the one to slip the note under his room door. Somehow the vigilantes had found out.

There was movement beside him and Jesse said, 'Ghastly sight, ain't it? A man hangin' there like that, all blown up and startin' to stink.'

'Why?' Ford asked, an edge to his voice.

'Conspiracy to commit murder,' Jesse said by way of explanation.

With a derisive snort, Ford said, 'Who?'

'Me,' stated a new voice.

Ford turned to look at the speaker. It was Wakefield. 'Why would he conspire to kill you?'

'The man had been causing trouble

for a while,' Wakefield lied. 'We had suspicions he was tied in with a lawless element that we've been having trouble with. We heard from a local that he was preparing to leave and when I approached him about it last night, he pulled a knife and tried to stab me with it.'

'So you hung him,' Ford said in disgust. 'What about a trial? Didn't he deserve one?'

'He had his trial,' Wakefield explained. 'Right then and there. We can't have members of the public stabbing officials of the law now, can we? So he was tried and found guilty. There was never any doubt.'

'Let's get one thing straight,' Ford spoke in an acidic tone. 'You fellers aren't the law. You're just a pack of killers posing as the law. Vigilantes who are no better than killers themselves.'

His gaze turned steely-cold as he looked Wakefield in the eye. 'And you sure as hell ain't no judge.'

Jesse grasped at the butt of his six-gun, a snarl on his face. The action was stopped cold as Ford's Peacemaker seemed to leap into his hand, his thumb eared back the hammer as it came level. Jesse froze, shock visible on his face at the deputy marshal's gun speed.

'I'd let that there hog-leg go friend or I'm liable to plaster your guts all over the street,' Ford warned him.

Jesse let the gun go as if his hand had been burned.

'Now that's better,' Ford approved. He turned to Wakefield. 'I was plannin' on ridin' out today to continue my search elsewhere. But not now. Somethin' stinks around here and I aim to find out what it is. And get that body down.'

Wakefield opened his mouth to speak, but Ford turned his back and strode off.

Cold eyes watched him go and when he was out of earshot Wakefield said harshly, 'He goes. I don't care how you do it, but I want him gone before tomorrow morning.'

Wakefield stormed off and Jesse

became aware of a presence beside him. He turned and saw Gil.

'Let me have a crack at him, Jesse,' he said, 'I always wanted to notch me up a lawman.'

'I don't know, Gil,' Jesse said hesitantly, remembering his brush with death, 'he's mighty fast.'

'So am I,' Gil boasted.

It was true, Gil was the fastest of all the vigilantes. Much faster than Jesse.

'All right,' he agreed. 'Do it.'

8

Ford spent the rest of a very long day asking many questions but received no answers in return. Everyone he spoke to took one look at his badge, became very nervous and remained tight-lipped. The more they refused to answer questions, the more frustrated Ford became. The men who followed him about town did not go unnoticed by him. Always at a distance, but they never tried to hide the fact.

Finally fed-up, Ford decided he needed a drink and stopped off at the Cedar Log.

He pushed in through the double doors and felt the whole barroom grow instantly tense.

His many years in the marshal service had taught him to be observant, especially when his life depended on it.

He knew from a quick glance that

96

there were roughly twenty men and five sporting women in the establishment. That the stairway to his left climbed to a first-floor landing which held a lounge occupied by a woman and a man. He also knew that there was a side door on the right with wall lamps either side and at one time the chandelier hanging from the ceiling had been shot-up, most likely by a drunken cowboy.

Nervous gazes followed him across the sawdust-covered plank floor as he bellied up to the long hardwood bar.

Behind the bar was a long double shelf stacked with bottles and glasses. A fat barkeep made his way along the bar and was about to ask Ford what his poison was when he glanced over Ford's shoulder and paled. The piano player who'd been belting out a tune found his fingers having trouble finding the right keys.

Ford didn't have to look around to work out what had just happened. He guessed the men who'd been following him all day had walked through the doors.

A great silence descended on the room and Ford levelled his gaze directly at the barkeep and said, 'Get me a beer.'

The man's mouth opened to say something, but whatever it had been never came out. Instead, it was interrupted by Gil's voice.

'You won't be needin' that drink, Ford,' he said confidently. 'Not where you're goin'.'

Ford turned to face Gil who was in the process of sweeping back the right side of his coat so his six-gun was easily accessible.

'Did Mordecai send you to do his dirty work for him?' Ford asked casually.

Gil frowned at the use of the Vigilante leader's name.

'Yeah,' Ford confirmed. 'I know who he is. And I'm guessin' that the son of a bitch is too gutless to do his own killin'.'

Gil ignored the comment and said, 'Jesse reckons you're fast. How fast?'

'I'm still alive,' Ford answered.

'Not for much longer,' Gil smiled coldly. 'Now how about we get this show started.'

Ford straightened and moved away from the bar. As he did so, he unhooked the hammerthong on the Peacemaker. He stopped and stood with his feet roughly shoulder width apart and waited as people around him scattered, trying to clear the line of fire.

'I'm goin' to kill you, lawdog,' Gil sneered.

'Have you ever heard of a man named Zachariah Hayes?' Ford asked him nonchalantly.

Gil pulled a face. 'Who?'

'Exactly,' Ford said and started his draw.

The Peacemaker came up so fast it was almost invisible to the naked eye. The cold black muzzle belched flame and before Gil could blink he had two slugs hammered into his chest.

The half-drawn Colt fell from lifeless fingers and dropped back into its holster.

The impact of the bullets punched him back, causing him to overbalance and stagger into a jumble of chairs and tables. With a loud clatter, he fell amongst them, knocking a table on to its side and upending two chairs.

The dying man stiffened and his boots drummed on the plank floor as his life finally ended. It was brief, bloody and violent. But that was the west. It was a bloody and violent place where men died every day.

Ford kept the Peacemaker trained on the downed man for a moment after he'd stopped moving then slipped it back into his holster.

The echo of the shots died away quickly and was replaced by a shocked and heavy silence, as every person in the room stared at the body of the dead vigilante.

The saloon doors flew open and five more vigilantes entered, led by Jesse. All were armed with either rifles or cut-off shotguns. One look at the body on the floor was all they needed for them to point their weapons at Ford.

'One of you fellers check Gil,' Jesse ordered without taking his eyes from Ford. 'Looks to me you might be in a little trouble, friend.'

'It was him or me,' Ford pointed out. 'And besides, you fellers ain't law in this town. Or anywheres else for that matter. The only law here is me so you might want to put them guns away and get both yourselves and your friend outta here.'

Jesse shook his head. 'You may wear a badge, but around here it ain't goin' to do you no good. The only law in this town is us so you'd best drop the gun belt and we'll take us a little walk.'

'I don't think so,' Ford grated.

'I do,' Jesse said cocking the twin hammers of the cut-off shotgun he carried.

It was right about then that Ford began to wish he'd never sent Tolliver off to do what he was doing.

★ ★ ★

The iron door slammed shut behind Ford with a loud clang. Silently he looked around at the small cell, complete with cot and waste bucket in the corner.

Ford turned back to look into the cold, hard face of Jesse. He could see the enjoyment hidden behind the mask.

'What now?' Ford asked.

Jesse shrugged nonchalantly. 'The Judge will come and see you and then we'll hang you. Quite simple really.'

'Is that what happened to the others?' Ford inquired.

'Yes and no.'

Anger blossomed within Ford but he never let it show. 'What do you mean?'

'We hung one and the other was ambushed by some passing stranger,' Jesse explained. 'We never did find out who it was.'

'You mean one of your lot shot him,' Ford surmised.

Jesse just looked at him and shrugged his shoulders.

'Why?' Ford asked. 'Why kill them?'

'Because they were in the way,' came the voice from the doorway of the rear cell block.

Ford's cold stare shifted from Jesse to Wakefield. 'In the way of what?'

'In the way of what we are doing in this town.'

After a brief moment to digest what he'd been told, Ford shook his head. 'I don't buy it. There has to be more. You don't just murder two marshals just because they are in the way. The second one maybe. But the first one must have been getting' close to somethin'. What was it?'

The was a small flicker in Wakefield's expression. Not much, but it told Ford he was right.

'Like I said,' Wakefield dismissed the suggestion, 'they were in the way.'

'So what about me? What do you have planned? You know once I disappear that the marshals ain't just goin' to sit back and take it. Old Bass will send every man he can spare into this country.'

'I have thought about that,' Wakefield allowed. 'But once the marshals find out how you were drunk, had an altercation with a deputy and it led to you shooting him down in cold blood, I'm sure they will be happy to see you hang.'

'Thought of everythin', huh?'

Wakefield looked pleased with himself. 'Pretty much.'

'So when is the big day?'

'Consider this to be your trial. You'll be hung the day after tomorrow.'

Ford was surprised and couldn't help but show it. 'I actually get a trial?'

Wakefield nodded. 'But don't get your hopes up. You'll still hang.'

'Was there even any doubt?'

* * *

'That just had to be the best breakfast I've eaten in a long while,' Tolliver said as he pushed the empty plate away from himself. He was certain that if he wasn't in company he'd probably lick the plate clean.

'Would you like some more coffee, Marshal Tolliver?' Nora Galloway asked, smiling warmly.

Tolliver offered the middle-aged woman his cup. 'Don't mind if I do, ma'am.'

'Are you moving on today, Marshal?' Leander Galloway asked.

Tolliver nodded and took a sip of the bitter-hot liquid. He swallowed and said, 'Yeah, I aim to ride into town today and meet up with Marshal Ford.'

'You will be careful, won't you?' Nora warned him. 'Those men are ghastly creatures. Every time Leander goes to town I worry sick that he might not come home.'

'You worry too much woman,' Galloway told his wife.

Tolliver had arrived at the Galloways' homestead the day before, and after their insistence, had stayed the night but had slept in the barn. The homestead was five or so miles from Stay and most of it was flat land beside the Moose River. Their story was the same as others he'd talked to. They only went to town when necessary and kept to themselves.

They had never met the two missing marshals, but there were rumours. Apparently, one of them had been hung and the other supposedly shot by an unknown person. Everything that happened in Stay was to do with the vigilance committee.

'I'll be careful, ma'am,' Tolliver said with a smile in an attempt to reassure her. 'If I run into any trouble I'll get out of town double-quick.'

Nora smiled thinly, knowing that Tolliver was trying to placate her.

The sound of drumming hoofs grew loud as a rider entered the yard at a good clip. Nora looked out of the window of the kitchen then turned her concerned gaze to her husband.

'It's Alvin,' she told her husband, mentioning their neighbour by his first name. 'Something is wrong.'

Galloway climbed to his feet closely followed by Tolliver. Both men hurried out the door and met the rail-thin man as he stepped up on to the veranda.

'What brings you ridin' in here like the hounds of hell were chasin' you, Alvin?' Galloway asked.

'There's murder afoot in the town this very mornin',' the man blurted out. 'They hung the clerk from the hotel, they did. And then there was trouble in the saloon and the marshal that arrived in town shot one of the vigilantes dead. Now they plan on hangin' him for it. They're callin' it murder.'

'They what?' Tolliver snapped.

Alvin looked at Tolliver wide-eyed. 'You heard me. They're goin' to hang him tomorrow.'

'The hell they are,' Tolliver snarled. 'There ain't no way in Hades that I'm about to let Ford swing.'

It was then that Alvin noticed the badge pinned to Tolliver's shirt. 'But what can you do? There's over a dozen of them?'

'I'll think of somethin',' Tolliver said gruffly.

9

Tolliver rode along the Main Street of Stay a little before noon, showing off his shiny marshal's badge as bold as brass. Almost every one of the town's citizens who saw him stopped and stared nervously at the big buckskin-clad man.

Though it wasn't their attentions that caught his eye. It was the bearded men in black that had him on edge. He made sure to keep his hand away from his six-gun as he rode so as not to provoke an unwanted incident.

Eventually, Tolliver found what he was after and drew his horse to a stop outside the Stay jail. He dismounted and tied the horse to a partially rotted hitch-rail, after which, he climbed the steps to the boardwalk and crossed to the jail door.

Tolliver was about to place his hand

upon the knob to turn it when the door swung open and yet another bearded man in black greeted him with what would appear to be disdain.

The man looked at the badge pinned to Tolliver's chest and asked, 'Is there somethin' I can do for you, Marshal?'

The man's sudden appearance had forced Tolliver to take a couple of steps back. 'I heard you had a friend of mine locked up in your jail. Do you mind tellin' me why?'

Jesse looked him over and said, 'He killed a man in cold blood. The Judge aims to hang him tomorrow.'

Tolliver cocked an eyebrow. 'In cold blood you say?'

Jesse nodded. 'Uh huh. Got witnesses that testified to that fact.'

'I bet,' Tolliver said skeptically.

'Listen,' Jesse started, his tone sharp, 'it don't matter if he's a marshal or not. Any man who guns down another in *cold blood* deserves to get the rope.'

Tolliver became aware of more vigilantes starting to gather either side of them. Five of them.

Holding his hands up in front of himself, Tolliver said, 'Just hold up there, friend. I ain't disbelievin' you. If you got witnesses that tell it that way, then he deserves to hang. But before I leave I'd still like to see him.'

The jail door swung open once more and another man stepped out into the morning light.

'Let him come in Jesse,' the man told him. 'I don't see a problem with it.'

'Are you sure, Judge?' Jesse queried.

'I'm sure it'll be fine,' Wakefield said, not taking his eyes from Tolliver.

The big man made to move forward towards the jail door when Wakefield added, 'Just as soon as he gives you his gun.'

Tolliver froze and his icy gaze cut into Wakefield. He let it linger for a moment before he shrugged his broad shoulders and said, 'OK.'

He hesitated as his hand started to drop towards his six-gun. Instead of drawing it, Tolliver moved both hands to the front and unbuckled the gun belt.

Handing it to Jesse, Tolliver pushed past two vigilantes and followed Wakefield into the office.

'You'll find him through there,' Wakefield pointed toward the door at the rear of the office.

'Your friend outside says you plan on hangin' him tomorrow,' Tolliver stated.

'That's right,' replied Wakefield.

'Kinda sudden, ain't it?'

'So is the way he killed the man in the saloon,' Wakefield countered.

'What about a trial?' Tolliver asked.

'Had it last evening after he committed the murder,' Wakefield informed him.

'Did he get fair representation?'

'He got what he deserved,' Wakefield snapped, tiring of the questions. 'Do you want to see him or not?'

Tolliver nodded and walked across to the door. He opened it and walked through.

Ford was surprised to see him but

didn't let it show. He remained silent, waiting for Tolliver to speak.

'Looks as though you've got yourself in a bit of a fix,' the big man observed.

'You could say that,' Ford answered as he looked over Tolliver's shoulder and watched Wakefield enter the cell block.

'I told you that temper of yours was goin' to get you into trouble one day,' Tolliver scolded. 'And look where you are now. Sittin' in this here cell waitin' for the hangman to come. You are one dumb son of a bitch.'

'How about you just shut the hell up and get me outta here,' Ford snapped.

Tolliver shook his head. 'Sorry, no can do. After the Judge here told me what happened I tend to agree with him. I guess you're goin' to hang.'

'Well, what in thunderation are you doin' here then?'

'I don't rightly know,' Tolliver shrugged. 'I might stick around and see you hang. It seems the least I can do after that low down dirty trick you pulled on me in

Helena. Kickin' a man there. It ain't right.'

Ford's eyes grew hard. 'If you ain't here to help me, you big son of a bitch, then get the hell out.'

Tolliver smiled. 'I'll be sure to say hello to Bass for you when I see him in Bozeman.'

There it was, Bass was nowhere near Bozeman. This told Ford that Tolliver was going nowhere and was going to hang around and try to get him out of the fix he was in.

'You do that,' Ford spat.

Tolliver turned away from the cell and stopped briefly on his way out to look at Wakefield and say, 'He's all yours.'

Ford watched the big man leave and noticed the smile of satisfaction on Wakefield's face. All he could do now was wait and hope that Tolliver was good enough to get him out. If he wasn't, they'd both be dead men.

* ★ ★

All eyes were on Tolliver when he rode out of Stay. Especially those of the two vigilantes who followed him for two miles along the trail. At that point, they stopped and watched him disappear over a low rise before they turned their mounts back to town.

Once he was out of sight, Tolliver eased his horse off the rutted trail and into a dense stand of conifers. When he figured he was far enough in to remain hidden from prying eyes, he dismounted and settled down to wait for dark.

Tolliver thought twice about a small fire but decided not to risk it. He needed the vigilantes to think he had indeed left. That way he was more likely to be able to slip back into Stay under the cover of darkness and remain undiscovered. He hoped.

The other problem he faced was the blue roan that Ford rode. The savage beast was pretty much a one-man horse and sometimes not even that as Ford could attest to. Why he kept him

114

Tolliver never knew, but Ford insisted that the spiteful animal was the best he'd ever had.

When Tolliver had asked him where he'd got the animal from Ford had just said, 'A dead man.'

Which was true. Ford had killed the horse's previous owner, a notorious outlaw named Harvey Black, in a town called Hell's End.

Anyway, he'd worry about that at the time. If need be, he'd steal another horse and leave the roan there.

* * *

It was after midnight when Tolliver finally slipped back into Stay. Under a shroud of darkness punctuated by faint starlight and a half-moon, the big man cautiously led his horse into town through a series of back alleyways until he came upon the livery. He left his horse tied to a corral rail and with as little noise as possible, entered the livery.

Inside, the stables were lit by the false light of a lantern. He found the blue roan and talked softly to the animal, hoping to sweet-talk it into behaving. As soon as he entered the stall with the saddle, the ill-tempered beast tried to take a piece out of Tolliver's hide with its teeth. However, he'd been expecting it and avoided the animal's jaws.

Next, up it lashed out with a powerful kick. Again Tolliver was able to avoid the blow.

'Damn it horse, let up,' Tolliver cursed the animal.

The roan snorted and tried to bite him again, this time, it let out a high-pitched, cranky squeal.

'Will you shut up,' Tolliver whispered harshly. 'If you get me caught then there is no way I can get Ford outta that damned jail and the bastards will hang him.'

At the mention of Ford's name, the roan's ears pricked and he suddenly quieted.

'That's better,' Tolliver said, relieved.

'Now stand still while I get this saddle on you.'

To Tolliver's surprise, the roan stood rock still while he saddled him. Then once he was done the big man said, 'I'm goin' to leave you here while I go and get Ford out of jail. Don't go anywhere.'

The roan snorted in response to his words and Tolliver shook his head at the thought that the animal had actually understood what he'd just said.

Tolliver let himself out of the livery and used the shadows to walk up on the jail. Twice he stopped for patrols. Just melted back into the shadows to remain unseen until the danger had passed.

When he reached the jail he quietly slipped into the darkened alley between it and the Stay bank. From there, Tolliver worked his way along the alley, feeling his way, guided by the rough wood of the jail wall, and around the back.

All was quiet, inside nothing seemed to move. Tolliver crept up to a barred window that he'd noticed when he visited Ford. He stood under it for what seemed like an age. Waiting, listening.

'Psssttt,' he hissed. 'Ford.'

Tolliver waited in silence then tried again, this time, a little louder.

'Will you shut up,' came Ford's harsh whisper. 'You might just as well blow a damned bugle.'

'Fine, I'll just leave you there and see how you get on,' Tolliver retorted.

'Whatever,' Ford said dismissively. 'Get me the hell outta here.'

'How many of them in there?'

'Only two, I think,' Ford answered.

'What is your plan?'

'Front door.'

Ford thought about it then said, 'Yeah, makes sense. That way hopefully you don't draw too much attention. If you put on a diversion it would probably have the opposite effect. All right, do it. And good luck.'

Tolliver made his way back along the alley and stopped just inside its dark opening. He paused and waited. When he was sure it was all clear he drew his six-gun and climbed the steps on to the jail veranda.

He walked quickly through the dim lantern light, his boot heels sounding unbelievably loud on the boards.

Tolliver grasped the door handle and turned it. He then gently put weight upon it and it opened a crack. *Good,* he thought, *at least it wasn't locked.*

He cocked the hammer of his gun, took a deep breath, swung the door wide and stepped through.

10

The two vigilantes inside were taken completely by surprise when Tolliver entered the jail, his fist full of Colt. They had been lounging in the office chairs when the door opened.

'What the hell?' gasped the first vigilante. 'You left.'

'And now I'm back,' Tolliver snapped. 'So shut up and get on your feet.'

Both men stood and Tolliver noticed that they didn't wear black coats.

'Isn't that somethin',' he said, voice dripping with sarcasm. 'You fellers don't wear the same clothes after all.'

'What now?' asked the vigilante who'd spoken before.

'We go out the back and let the marshal out. One wrong move and I'll plug the pair of you,' Tolliver said. The last piece of information he directed at the second vigilante. The quiet, scarred-face one. The one who looked to Tolliver like he would be the bravest.

Tolliver waved the gun in the direction of the cells. 'Start walkin'.'

Once through the door, the two men stopped and Tolliver asked them, 'Where are the keys?'

The vigilante who did the talking pointed silently to a hook on the wall beside the doorway.

Satisfied, Tolliver went through a series of fluid movements in which he brought the barrel of his six-gun crashing down on the back of the quiet vigilante's head. With a grunt, the man buckled at the knees.

He didn't stop there, though. Tolliver continued quickly and before the second vigilante could register his alarm, he too was falling to the cold hard floor.

Ford watched silently and had to give the big man his due, he was someone to count on in a tight situation. He grasped the steel bars of the cell door as Tolliver grabbed the keys and unlocked it. When he swung it open, the door screeched loudly.

'Thanks,' Ford said. 'Now let's get the hell outta here.'

The pair hurried out into the office and Ford strode across to a tall cabinet along the left side wall.

'What in tarnation are you doin'?' Tolliver asked urgently.

'Guns.'

'What?'

'I'm gettin' my guns,' Ford explained.

'Well hurry up.'

Finding what he was looking for, Ford strapped the Peacemaker on and scooped up the Winchester. He crossed the room to where Tolliver stood by the door.

'Where are the horses?' he asked him.

'At the livery,' Tolliver informed Ford. 'And before you say anythin' I didn't think it would be wise to bring the broncs down here and tie them up outside. Especially that man-eater you ride.'

Without another word, the two men

stepped out of the jail and walked right into trouble.

* * *

'Hey, what the hell is goin' on here?' the vigilante blurted out from the top of the steps on the boardwalk.

He suddenly realized who Ford was and clawed for his gun. He had it half drawn when both Ford's and Tolliver's six-guns roared together.

The impact of the slugs punched the black-clad man backward off the boardwalk and he landed with a sickening thud on his back in the dirt. The sound of the gunfire echoed along the street like some loud tolling of a giant bell signalling danger.

Shouts soon started to fill Stay's main street and the semi-darkness came alive with moving figures.

'This way,' Tolliver urged Ford and the pair ducked into the darkened alley.

Keeping to the shadows at the rear of the buildings as much as possible, they were able to reach the livery unseen.

'Your horse is in its stall with your saddle on him,' Tolliver informed Ford.

'How did you manage that?'

'It weren't easy, trust me. But we had words and reached an understandin'.'

When Ford found the roan he was never so happy to see the cantankerous beast. He let him out of the stall and started to lead him towards the back of the stables when Tolliver came in leading his own mount.

'We got a problem out there,' he warned Ford. 'Some of them vigilante fellers are comin' up on the stables.'

'How many?'

'Three maybe.'

'We'll have to go out the front way,' Ford stated.

They led the animals to the double front doors and paused just long enough for Tolliver to stick his head out to see if it was clear. As soon as he did, there was a shout then the thunder of six-guns. A staccato sound hammered upon the plank doors as slugs impacted and chewed splinters from them.

'I guess that way is out,' Ford guessed.

'They got us trapped like fish in a damned barrel,' Tolliver cursed.

'Did you see how many there were?'

'Four or five.'

'If we stay here they'll burn the place to the ground to get us out,' Ford surmised. 'The only thing to do is try and bust out.'

Tolliver nodded. 'Yeah, you could be right.'

'All right, let's do it.'

'Before we go,' Tolliver stopped him, 'there is a place about five miles out on the Moose River. The folks there are named Galloway.'

Another volley of gunfire hammered into the door.

Tolliver continued, 'If we get separated I'll meet you there.'

Ford nodded. 'Mount up. I'll hook a rope to the door and pull it open. That way we're both in the saddle.'

Ford tied the rope to the door and

climbed aboard the roan. He looped the end of it around the saddle-horn a couple of times and drew his Peacemaker.

'Are you ready?' he asked Tolliver.

'Now is as good a time as any,' the big man confirmed.

Ford backed his horse up until the door came open, then quickly released the rope and let it fall. A loud 'Heyaa!' sounded and Tolliver heeled his mount forward with a savage kick.

The horse hit the main street running and gunfire erupted as they tried to bring him down. Ford followed suit and the blue roan lunged forward when he gave it a kick. The next instant he was out on the street and angry lead hornets buzzed about his head.

Ford turned the roan to the left and after firing a couple of shots followed Tolliver.

Loud shouts and gunfire filled his cars. He felt the passage of a bullet tear through his shirt and another singe the skin of his cheek.

A hard kick sent the roan into a maddened run. Ahead, Ford could see Tolliver just about to pass beyond the town boundary and he genuinely thought that they were going to make it unscathed. Two things happened to change that.

First, he saw Tolliver topple from the back of his racing mount. The second was the impact of a slug in his side which felt like he'd been kicked by a mule.

Ford grasped at the saddle horn as he desperately tried to stay in the saddle. The Colt Peacemaker fell from his grip and was left in the dust while the roan raced on, its rider wobbling in the saddle.

The gunfire died away as he reached the edge of town. Ford dragged the roan to a stop and looked down at Tolliver. The big man was still alive and moving, albeit not a lot.

'I'm hit, Gus,' he told Tolliver. 'Are you able to get up? If you can I might be able to get you up behind me.'

A low moan was accompanied by a rattling cough.

'I'm done for, Josh' Tolliver gasped. 'I been hit in the lungs. I won't see daylight. You get out. The Galloways. Head there.'

'If I can get you on the horse, we can find a place to doctor you,' Ford said, a hint of desperation in his voice.

For us both, Ford thought as fire ripped through his side.

'Damnit, Ford. Just go. I'm dead anyway. No . . . ' a bolt of pain ripped through Tolliver's body and he bit off the rest of the sentence.

'I'm sorry, Gus,' Ford grated.

'Me too. Now git.'

Gunfire erupted as vigilantes closed in behind him, their bullets once more snapping close overhead. Ford gave Tolliver one last look then set the roan into a run, a mile-eating gait that would carry him clear of the danger behind him.

'Good luck, Ford,' Tolliver whispered as the drum of hoofbeats died away.

He felt around until he found his Colt which he'd lost in the fall, but surprisingly it was beside him. He smiled faintly, and a thin trickle of blood slid from the corner of his mouth. His breathing grew laboured.

Tolliver lay there in pain for what seemed like an age before the vigilantes started to gather around him.

'He's still alive, Jesse,' one of them said and poked at Tolliver with his boot. 'It's that other damned marshal that rode out of here.'

As his strength waned, Tolliver gathered what remained and lifted the Colt. The man that had nudged him froze, his mouth open. Then the six-gun bucked in Tolliver's hand and the slug it spewed took off the top of the vigilante's head.

The others grabbed frantically for their guns but there was no need. Tolliver had used all of his strength for that one shot.

'What the hell is goin' on?' Wakefield shouted as he arrived on the scene. He looked down and saw the body of the dead vigilante. His voice grew cold. 'Why is Barrett lyin' there dead?'

'There was a jailbreak,' Jesse informed him and pointed at the dying Tolliver. 'This feller here helped Ford escape.'

On closer inspection, Wakefield saw who it was. 'You were gone. Why did you return?'

Tolliver coughed weakly and said, 'You don't th . . . think I was g . . . goin' to leave F . . . Ford with scum like you?'

Wakefield's face turned ugly as he reached into his long coat and drew his six-gun. It was a .45 caliber, Schofield. He cocked it and pointed it at the prone figure on the ground.

Tolliver smiled. If it had been bright enough, the small gathering of killers would have seen his blood-stained teeth.

'Go ahead,' Tolliver grated. 'You gutless piece of . . . '

The sound of the Schofield rolled along the street funneled by the lines of buildings. Tolliver died with the last word on his lips as the slug punched into his skull.

Wakefield let his eyes linger on the body for a moment before he nodded with satisfaction, then looked at his men until his gaze landed on Jesse.

'Get some men after Ford,' he commanded. 'I want him found. If you have to kill him, then do it. But he doesn't get away. If he does, I'll hang those responsible. We are on a good thing here and I won't let any of you damned fools wreck it.'

Wakefield turned away before Jesse could say anything else, then he was gone.

'Five of you get after Ford,' Jesse ordered. 'The rest of you get Barrett off the street.'

★ ★ ★

Pain and loss of blood caused Ford to lose all track of time and distance. At first, the darkness was filled with looming shadows and the outlines of moving objects flying past as the roan galloped on.

After a while, his mind began to drift and he had trouble focusing. The roan sensed something was wrong and slowed its pace to try and keep its rider aboard.

The trail climbed a small hill and as they topped it, Ford managed to make out a faint light in the distance. A beacon guiding them onwards.

'The light, feller,' Ford mumbled to the horse. 'We gotta go to the light.'

The roan moved forward at a walk as if knowing what it needed to do.

11

The muffled snort of a horse brought Nora Galloway awake as the sun was poking its head up over the horizon to bathe the valley in its golden glow. Leander had been up all night with a foaling mare and hadn't come to bed until the early hours.

It was then that she noticed the lantern burning in the living room. A quick glance beside her told Nora that Leander must have forgotten to put it out.

The muffled snort came again. She frowned and climbed out of bed. The nightgown Nora wore fell to just above the floor when she stood up. She crossed to the window and looked outside.

She gasped audibly when she saw a horse she'd never seen before standing in her yard. Beside it, laying face down in the dirt was a man.

Nora hurried across to the bed and shook her husband awake.

'Leander,' she said urgently. 'Leander, wake up.'

'What is it?' he mumbled drowsily.

'There's a man in the yard.'

'What?'

'There's a man in the yard,' she said again. 'Get up. I think he's hurt.'

The fog of sleep was swept away as Leander sat up.

'What?'

Nora grabbed him by the arm and dragged him to the window. 'There, see.'

Leander held his frown for a long moment and turned away from the window. He pulled on some clothes and walked from the bedroom, through the dining area to the sitting room and opened the front door.

Before he stepped out on to the veranda, he reached up to the double pegs above the doorway and took down a Winchester he kept there.

'Wait here,' he told his wife and went out, closing the door behind himself.

Warily, Galloway approached the fallen rider. He waited to see any indication of movement. His eyes scanned the surrounding landscape looking for any sign of ambush but nothing moved.

Galloway knelt down beside the body and rolled it over. The man's jacket fell open and revealed two things. The bloody wound in the man's side and a United States Deputy Marshal's badge.

The man moaned.

'Nora!' Galloway shouted back at the house. 'Quickly, come and give me a hand!'

Nora Galloway appeared on the veranda. 'What is it?'

'Come and give me a hand,' Galloway said more calmly this time.

Nora ran across to him. 'What's wrong?'

'I'm afraid, something terrible,' Galloway surmised. 'Look at his chest.'

Nora saw the badge. 'Oh lord.'

'Help me get him inside.'

'I need to fetch Doc Jones,' Galloway told his wife. 'That bullet needs to come out.'

Nora turned away from where Ford lay on the bed. She'd begun to bathe the wound in his side but knew her husband was right, even if she didn't like the thought of him riding to town.

'You be careful, Leander Galloway,' she cautioned him. 'You know how I worry when you go there.'

'I'll be fine,' he reassured her. 'I've hidden his horse, but if you have any trouble you know where the rifle is.'

She watched nervously as he left, already anxious that he might not return. A moan from Ford diverted her attention back to him.

Nora moved back to his side and continued to clean the wound.

★ ★ ★

Mid-morning, when Galloway arrived in Stay, the town was quieter than usual and he put it down to whatever had happened the previous night. He didn't have to ride far to find out why.

When he passed the undertakers, Galloway saw the open upright coffin. It was occupied by Gus Tolliver and still pinned to his chest, for all the town to see was his marshal's badge.

Galloway turned his gaze away from the macabre sight. It was hard to believe that he could be talking and sharing a meal with a man one day and the next day see him dead.

Riding on, the homesteader found the doctor's house. Galloway was about to guide his horse over to the hitch-rail when he noticed that he was being watched.

Weighing up what to do, Galloway decided to pull up at the hitch-rail anyway. Once there, he dismounted and tied the reins off. Then he walked through the opening in the picket fence and along the dirt path that led to the steps.

He was about to climb them when

the door opened and doctor Eli Jones emerged. He was a wiry middle-aged man with greying hair.

'Saw you comin',' he explained to Galloway. 'What can I do for you, Leander?'

Galloway paused and then said, 'I got myself a carbuncle, Doc. It needs some attention.'

'Whereabouts is it?'

'Umm,' Galloway looked about and saw the vigilante still watching him. 'Umm . . . Well, it's here.'

Galloway started unbuckling his belt.

'Whoa there, Leander,' Jones said, holding up a wrinkled hand. 'I don't think this is an appropriate place to be dropping your drawers.'

Galloway looked about innocently. 'You could be right, Doc. I think we'd best go inside.'

'I agree,' Jones said grimly.

Once inside and the door closed, Doc Jones showed Galloway along a narrow hallway, past a number of closed doors and out into a well-lit back room.

'This should do,' Jones said. 'OK, Leander, get them off.'

'I don't need to, Doc,' Galloway said quietly, 'there ain't nothin' wrong with me.'

'There what?' Jones said, his face starting to redden.

'There is somethin' wrong, Doc, just not with me,' Galloway informed him. 'I'm sorry I lied, but there was one of The Judge's men across the street watchin' us.'

Jones nodded. 'I did happen to notice that. Is it Nora?'

'What? No, no,' Galloway assured him. 'I got a wounded man out at my place. Got a slug lodged in him and it needs to come out.'

The doctor stiffened at the news.

'Who is the man?' Jones asked warily, knowing that he may not like the answer.

He was right.

'It's the marshal, Ford, I think his name is.'

Jones closed his eyes for a moment

while he let it sink in.

'You do know what will happen if they find out that he's at your place, don't you?'

'I saw the pine box when I rode in,' Galloway said through gritted teeth. 'The big feller, the marshal, his name was Tolliver. I had supper with him the other night. Now he's dead. I ain't about to let that happen to another one. If you don't want to come and dig that slug out then at least tell me how to.'

'I didn't say I wasn't coming, Leander. I just wanted to know if you understood what could happen if the vigilance committee finds out.'

'I'm fully aware of what could happen.'

'OK then. This is what we're going to do,' Jones stated. 'You leave for home now. I will follow you after a short while. Better still, go to the dry goods store or somewhere else and buy something. And limp. If you have a carbuncle and I've just lanced it, you would limp.'

Galloway nodded. 'Before I go, do you mind tellin' me what happened last night? Why I found a half-dead marshal in my yard this morning?'

'Apparently, the second marshal came back after he was supposed to leave,' Jones explained. 'He busted the other one out last night and killed two of The Judge's men doing it.'

'And so he's put him on display.'

'Yes,' Jones informed him.

Galloway nodded. 'I'd best be gone. I'll see you out at the homestead.'

'I'll be there around dark,' Jones stated. 'If he ain't dead by then, he will probably live.'

★ ★ ★

It wasn't long after noon when the thunder of hoofs coming into the yard startled Nora Galloway. When she looked out of the window she was more surprised to see five black-coated figures on top of the horses.

They drew up in the centre of the

141

yard and a small dust cloud drifted through the air after they stopped.

'Hey you in the house,' one of the men shouted. 'Come on out.'

Nora gathered herself and hurried to the front door. When she opened it she tried to look as calm as possible as she stepped out on to the veranda.

'What can I do for you, gentlemen?' Nora asked, a slight quiver in her voice.

The man in the centre of the group eased his mount forward and said, 'We're lookin' for an escaped prisoner ma'am.'

'Well he ain't here,' Nora told him.

'Then you won't mind if we look then.'

'I certainly do mind,' Nora snapped. 'You have no right here.'

'I have all the rights I need,' the man said firmly.

Nora watched as he motioned to one of the riders to go and check the house. Before he reached the veranda she hurried inside and took down the Winchester. No sooner had the man

142

climbed the steps, when he was looking down the barrel of the rifle.

'Get the hell off my land,' Nora snarled. Her eyes blazed.

The man stopped short, unsure of what to do next. Would the woman shoot? Maybe not, but he wasn't about to find out. He backed away.

'What are you doin'?' the leader of the group asked. Then he saw the rifle.

'Ma'am, you need to put the rifle away before you go and do somethin' silly,' he said cautiously.

'If any of you takes a step towards this house or in any other direction except towards the gate, I'm goin' to plug him,' Nora snarled.

'Do you think she means it, Lem?' one of the riders asked their leader.

'Of course she don't mean it,' Lem snapped and started to climb down from his horse.

Nora raised the rifle and squeezed off a shot. The rifle whip-lashed and Lem's low-crowned hat flew of his head and into the dirt. He froze, a thin bead of sweat starting to form on his brow.

'The next one goes an inch and a half lower,' Nora informed him. 'Now get, all of you. You don't belong here.'

Lem signalled to the dismounted man who walked back towards his horse. Then he turned his attention back to Nora.

'You won't get away with this,' he said coldly. 'Once The Judge finds out we'll be back and then you'll be for it.'

Nora remained silent as she watched them ride out of the yard and head west towards the undulating foothills. Once they were out of sight she dropped the rifle and fell to her knees. She clasped her hands to her face and wept loudly. She was still there an hour later when her husband came home.

12

'The bullet is out and he's still asleep,' Jones told Leander and Nora as he closed the bedroom door behind him and joined them in the dining room. 'Keep an eye on him just to make sure no infection sets in and I'll be back to check on him in a couple of days. If the wound does become infected, come and get me.'

'Are you sure you won't stay the night, Eli?' Nora asked him.

Outside, the inky darkness covered the land with its black blanket. Inside, the Galloway home was lit with kerosene lamps which cast their orange light about the dining room.

'Thank you Nora, but no,' he smiled softly. 'I have a plethora of patients to see in the morning so I must be getting back.'

'Be careful then,' Nora urged him.

'It should be I saying that to you,' Jones surmised. 'After all, it is you who will have the wrath of the vigilance committee come down upon you if they find the marshal here. Besides that, after what you did to them today I would be on your toes. They ain't likely to let it go easy.'

Nora nodded.

'Tell Mary I'll see her at the church on Sunday,' Nora said, mentioning the doctor's wife.

'I'll do that,' he said. 'I'll see myself out. I'll see you in a couple of days.'

After he was gone, Nora looked at her husband and said, 'I'm scared, Leander. After what happened today with those men.'

'We'll be fine,' he tried to reassure her and himself.

★ ★ ★

'They didn't find him, Mordecai,' Jesse said, knowing that his words would be unacceptable.

146

Wakefield's face grew taut. 'I told you never to call me that. If you do it when no one is around, it makes it more likely that you'll do it when someone is.'

'Sorry, Judge.'

'Where are they now?' he asked Jesse in a measured voice.

'Over at the Cedar Log gettin' somethin' to eat and havin' a drink,' Jesse explained. 'They'll head back out tomorrow. Mind you, he could be long gone by then.'

Wakefield shook his head. 'They go back out tonight. That son of a bitch will still be around somewhere. If I know him, he ain't goin' nowhere until this mess all goes away.'

'They're pretty wore out Judge . . .'

'I don't give a damn,' Wakefield snapped. 'Send out a different group, I don't care. Just find that damned marshal!'

'There is one other thing,' Jesse informed his boss.

'What?'

'The men were checkin' out a spread

today and a woman with a rifle run 'em off,' Jesse told him. 'Somethin' may need to be done about it.'

Wakefield waved the problem away. 'We'll worry about it after we get Ford back. Until then, it is all about that damned man.'

'Well, he can't have gone far, we're pretty sure he's got a bullet in him,' Jesse tried to sound positive.

Wakefield nodded. 'Keep an eye on the doctor. He might be the one to lead us to him if that is the case.'

★ ★ ★

Ford pushed the empty plate away from himself and smiled at Nora Galloway.

'That was a mighty fine supper, ma'am, thank you.'

'Are you sure you don't want some more?' she asked hesitantly, afraid he might say yes.

'No thanks. Two helpings of that stew is about all I can eat at the moment,' he smiled cheekily. 'Maybe when I'm feelin' a little better . . . '

'If you get to feeling any better I'm thinking that Leander may have to butcher a cow to feed you.'

Ford reddened a touch as he reached for a steaming cup of coffee.

He'd woken the morning after the doctor had tended his wound. Sore and stiff, but feeling OK. Now three days later he was out of bed and feeling good. His strength had mostly returned and so had the memory of that dreadful night.

Since then, Ford had vowed that Mordecai Wakefield and his men would pay the ultimate price for their murderous ways.

'I doubt even that would be enough, Nora,' Galloway stated. 'Not for a fit young man like the marshal.'

Suddenly there was a commotion outside and Ford dropped his hand reflexively to his hip and grasped nothing. He cursed silently. Nora looked worried as Galloway rose from the table and peered through the window out into the darkness.

'It's OK,' he told them. 'It's Doc Jones.'

Ford couldn't help but notice the relief on Nora's face.

'It's OK, ma'am,' he said, trying to relieve her anxieties. 'Once the doc tells me I'm fit enough I'll move on.'

'And go where?' Nora asked without thinking.

'I still have a job to do,' he reminded her.

Galloway opened the door and let the doctor in. He took one look at Ford and said, 'I see you are up and about.'

'Yes, thanks to you, Doc.'

'It's good to see you, Eli,' Nora greeted him. 'How's Mary?'

'Fine, Nora, she's fine.'

'Would you like a coffee? The pot is still hot.'

Jones nodded. 'I'll have it after I've examined the marshal here. Thank you. That would be great, I could use one.'

'I'll give your horse some water, Eli,' Galloway told him. 'Maybe some oats too.'

Galloway left and Jones started his examination of Ford.

'What is happenin' in town, Doc?' Ford asked.

'They're still tryin' to track you down, so I hear,' he informed him. 'They are of an opinion that you are wounded and somebody is sheltering you.'

Ford grew concerned. 'Are they watchin' you?'

'Not that I'm aware of.'

'Can you tell me what they did with Tolliver?' Ford asked him.

Jones' face screwed up in disgust. 'He's right where they left him. On display outside of the undertakers.'

'Damn him,' Ford cursed. 'When can I get back to ridin', Doc? I still got me a job to do.'

'The way you're healin' up, give it a couple of days, maybe three, and you should be right. That wound in your side is healing nicely with no sign of infection.'

That was something at least.

'How long has Mordecai Wakefield

151

been in town anyway?'

The doctor raised his eyebrows. 'Is that his name?'

'It sure is,' Ford answered. 'He's just a straight-up outlaw.'

'They've been here around six months,' Jones recalled. 'It was only a matter of days before Sheriff Milsom died and they took over running the law. Their law.'

'Law enforced with fear and subjugation?'

'That's about right,' Jones agreed with Ford's assessment.

'Say, you couldn't get a message out on the wire could you?'

Jones shook his head. 'Not a hope. The vigilantes have a man stationed in the telegraph office all of the time.'

'Then I guess it's up to me,' Ford said resignedly.

'Up to you to do what?'

'Stop them, Doc. Stop them.'

★ ★ ★

Two sets of eyes watched as Doctor Eli Jones returned home sometime after midnight. Hidden in the shadows, the two vigilantes waited until he'd gone inside his house before they went to find Jesse and tell him what they saw.

Ten minutes after they'd talked to him, Jesse was banging on the door to Wakefield's room. Inside, a whore stirred as the Vigilante moved her arm that was draped across his chest. The springs squeaked in protest as he climbed out of bed and picked up his six-gun from where it sat on a polished table.

'Who is it?' he grouched.

'It's me, Jesse.'

The door swung open and Jesse was faced with a cocked gun pressed into his middle. 'What the hell do you want at this time of night? A man should damn well shoot you.'

'We think we've found Ford,' he told Wakefield. 'Or someone who knows where he is.'

'Who?'

'The doc.'

Wakefield's eyes flickered as he thought quickly, then he smiled. A cold, cruel smile that could only mean one thing.

'Bring him to me. And his wife. We'll find out what he knows.'

* * *

Mary Jones sat sobbing in the corner of the room with a trembling hand held to her bruised right cheek. Her husband was tied to a chair in the centre of the room, his face bloody, skin torn and eyes swollen shut. He was unconscious and his breathing was laboured.

'What do you think?' Jesse asked his boss. 'He was a tough old bird. Do you think she told us the truth?'

Eli Jones had somehow remained silent throughout his interrogation. It was his wife who had eventually given them what they wanted after she'd been able to witness no more.

'I guess we'll find out,' Wakefield said.

Jesse snapped his fingers as a thought

popped into his head.

'I just remembered. That place she told us about is the same one where Lem and the others were run off the other day.'

Wakefield nodded and rubbed at his bruised knuckles. 'Makes sense. If he is there, bring them all in. We'll have ourselves a hangin' party. These damn people in this town are startin' to forget their place.'

'I'll send Lem, Talbot, Miller and a couple of others out to bring them in,' Jesse informed Wakefield.

Wakefield stared out the window at the sun as it poked its head over the distant mountains. He nodded. 'Get it done.'

★ ★ ★

Ford sat in the bright morning sunshine cleaning the Winchester, enjoying the warmth flooding his body. Before the doc had left last night, he'd told him a couple of days and already he was chomping at the bit. Mentally, he worked on how best to bring down Wakefield and his gang of killers.

Inside his mind, he'd killed the vigilante many times over, but in reality, it wouldn't be so easy.

The smell of freshly cooked bread suddenly wafted across the yard and made his stomach rumble. It was the second loaf Nora had cooked that morning while Galloway worked on a downed rail on the horse corral.

Inside the corral, the roan eyed the man carefully as he worked. Ford still couldn't believe that the beast had let Galloway peacefully lead him from the barn where he'd been hidden.

'Go figure,' Ford said to no one in particular.

Ford had begun to reload the Winchester with .45-.75 caliber cartridges when he stopped and cocked an ear. He wasn't sure what he'd heard at first and frowned. A distant rumbling.

He looked out across to the river to the mountains beyond half expecting to see a faint cloud of dust from a rock slide. But there was nothing except the rock walls of the tall peaks and the trees that climbed throughout the foothills.

And still, there was the sound of . . . hoof beats.

'Damn it,' Ford cursed and hurriedly stuffed the last of the cartridges into the rifle's magazine.

As the drumming grew louder, Galloway turned to look at Ford. He shouted across the yard. 'Riders comin' in?'

'That's what I figure. Have you got a gun?'

'It's in the barn.'

'You'd best get it,' Ford shouted back. 'I have a feelin' that this ain't a social visit.'

'Maybe you should hide inside before they get here,' Galloway suggested as he jogged into the barn.

'Nope,' Ford mumbled to himself as he worked the lever of the Winchester. 'I've had enough of hidin'. Now it's time to fight back.'

13

The five riders thundered into the yard to find Ford standing there waiting for them. They hauled back on their horse's reins and brought them to a hard stop.

It wasn't until the dust had mostly cleared that they could make out Galloway standing at the large entrance to the barn. He held his cocked rifle across his body in a non-threatening way towards the riders, but Galloway could bring it to bear with a minimum of fuss should he need to.

Ford waited until the bearded, black-coated riders had brought their stomping mounts under control before saying, 'I believe you fellers are lookin' for me?'

Lem swept back his jacket to expose the butt of his six-gun. The others did likewise.

'You're comin' with us, Ford,' he said with authority. 'We're takin' you back to hang. You and those that have helped you.'

'Well, that is certainly a good incentive to lay down this here rifle and throw my hands up, ain't it?' Ford's voice dripped with sarcasm. 'How did you find me?'

'The doc talked.'

Inside the house, Nora watched on nervously and a cold shiver ran down her spine upon hearing Lem's comment.

'You have overlooked the one simple thing that stands out in this equation,' Ford pointed out.

'What might that be?'

'You didn't bring enough men.'

Lem's jaw dropped when he realized what was about to happen. The Winchester in Ford's grip came up and leveled on the terrified vigilante. The rifle bucked in Ford's hands, and blue-grey gunsmoke erupted from the barrel, punctuated by flame.

The slug punched into Lem's chest and knocked him back over his horse's rump. By the time he hit the hard-packed earth with a sickening thump, he was dead.

While Lem was falling, the rest of the vigilantes were drawing their six-guns. Ford had shifted his aim and now the Winchester centered on Miller. While he'd been adjusting his aim, Ford had worked the lever and jacked another round into the breech.

The rifle roared again and Miller grunted audibly as the bullet hit him in his middle. Gut-shot, he slid sideways from the saddle on to the ground where he curled into a ball as the pain started to settle in.

The guns of the three remaining vigilantes were out and firing by now, and slugs cut the air close to Ford. They snapped loudly as they passed causing Ford to duck instinctively and drop to his knees. With all their attention on Ford, the surviving vigilantes forgot about Galloway. And now, after a rapid recovery from the brutality of the opening rounds, he too joined the fray.

A bullet from Galloway's gun cut close to one of the vigilantes who quickly swiveled in his saddle and snapped a shot at the homesteader. The slug chewed splinters from one of the barn doors and sprayed razor-sharp slivers through the air.

Galloway fired again and got second time lucky as the man threw his arms up and toppled from his horse.

Inside the house Nora watched it all unfold. The deafening gunfire, the men dying violently before her eyes, and out there amongst it all, her husband.

Her hand went to her throat. *Oh God. Please let him live.*

Now, after the short, vicious exchange of gunfire, there were two vigilantes left. One took stock of the situation and ran, leaving his *compadre* on his lonesome.

The remaining man sighted on Ford but a shot from Galloway smashed into his leg. He cried out in pain and his jerky reaction threw off his aim enough for the slug to fly high and right. Then the wounded man's horse lurched sideways and he became unseated.

The vigilante hit the ground hard beneath his flailing mount's legs. He rolled away from the deadly append-ages and came up on to one knee, his face a mask of pain and rage. Despite the fall, he still managed to retain his six-gun and now looked for a clear target.

Ford sighted on him and squeezed the trigger. The Winchester kicked back into his shoulder and his limited view through the gunsmoke at the end of the barrel saw the final vigilante fall.

As the final echoes of gunshots died away across the Moose River, Ford climbed to his feet and looked about the yard and realized there were no more threats.

'Galloway, are you alright?' he called across to the homesteader.

Galloway just stared silently at the men that lay in his yard.

'Galloway?'

His head snapped around. 'What? Oh, yeah. I'm fine.'

There was a moan from the wounded Miller. Ford trained his rifle on him and slowly approached the downed man. To his left, the screen door slammed back as Nora Galloway burst through it and began to run towards her husband.

'Don't come out here, Nora,' he cautioned her. 'You don't need to see this.'

But in her desperation she ignored him and threw her arms about her husband when she reached him, silently weeping as he wrapped her up.

Meanwhile, Ford knelt down beside the dying Miller. He rolled the man on to his back and moved his hands so he could see the wound. He looked at Miller and shook his head. 'There ain't nothin' I can do for you.'

'I . . . I kinda expected that.'

There was no animosity towards Ford from the dying man. Just a resignation of what was to come.

'Is the doctor still alive?' Ford asked Miller.

He nodded jerkily. 'Yeah.'

'Why is Wakefield in Stay?' Ford asked him. 'What is there for him?'

'We needed . . . a place to hole up for . . . a while,' Miller gasped. 'After that . . . job we done a while back.'

'What job?'

'Fifty thousand dollars in gold coin,' Miller answered.

Ford searched his memory for a moment and then he recalled the incident. Around seven months back a money shipment on a stage was hit. The $50,000 it carried was stolen and everyone was killed, the cavalry escort that accompanied the stage included.

'That was Wakefield?' Ford asked.

'Yeah,' Miller nodded and then gasped as a fresh wave of pain washed over him.

'Where's the money now?'

Miller smiled showing blood-stained teeth. 'Safe. He keeps . . . it in his room. Behind the sideboard.'

The vigilante stiffened and went still. His chest stopped the regular rise and fall of the living.

'Hey,' Ford shook him gently. 'Hey.'

It was no use. Miller was all talked out. All that remained was death.

A shadow fell across Ford and he looked up to see Galloway standing over him.

'He dead?'

Ford nodded.

'What are we goin' to do now?'

Ford rose to his feet and looked about. He thought for a moment then said, 'We need to get your wife somewhere safe before they come back.'

'I can send her over to the Wilson spread,' Galloway told him. 'She should be safe there for a while. What are we goin' to do?'

'After you help me, I need you to ride to Fort Somerset,' Ford explained. 'While you're gone I'll be keepin' Wakefield and his men busy.'

'You do realize that the ride is a four day round trip?' Galloway explained.

'Uh huh.'

'What makes you think that you can keep them busy for that long?'

Ford smiled wryly. 'I'm goin' to steal his money.'

* ★ ★

Talbot thundered into Stay on a worn-out, foam-lathered horse. He was bathed in sweat and when he dragged the mount to a shuddering stop at the hitch-rail, he just leaped from the saddle and left the horse standing where it was.

Townsfolk stopped and stared at the obviously panic-stricken man who rushed up the steps of the Cedar Log. He crashed his way through the front doors and looked about the mostly empty room. He scanned the tables and spotted Jesse at a corner one with Luther.

He hurried across to the table and scooped up the half empty bottle of rye and took a big swig. After which he slammed it back down on the battered tabletop.

Jesse could plainly see that all was not right.

'What happened?' he asked, his voice carried a hard edge.

Talbot's grey eyes locked on to Jesse's gaze. Beneath his dark beard was a pale shocked face.

'We found Ford,' he informed Jesse. 'By damn we found the bastard.'

'And?'

'And I'm all that's left!' Talbot half shouted. 'The son of a bitch opened up on us and cut the others down cold. Between him and that damned homesteader feller we didn't have a chance.'

'All right, take it easy,' Jesse said in an effort to calm him. 'Tell me what happened so I can pass it on to The Judge.'

'When we showed up at the homestead, Ford was just standin' out in the yard as bold as all get out,' Talbot told Jesse. His eyes widened as he continued, 'Lem told him we were takin' him in and then he just up and told Lem that he hadn't brought enough help. Then he just cut loose. I ain't never seen a man do that before. Not that quick. Not with a rifle. Lem and Miller were down before we could even get our guns drawn. That other marshal was right. He said Ford would come. And he said he'd kill us all.'

'Just calm down and stop gettin' all bent out of shape. What happened next?'

'The homesteader cut loose and they had us cold. There weren't nothin' we could do.'

'So how come you managed to get out?' Luther asked. 'You cut and run?'

'I did what I had to!' Talbot screeched and spittle flew from his lips.

All eyes in the saloon were suddenly directed at their table.

'OK, calm down,' Jesse snapped. 'Go and get yourself a drink.'

Talbot reached for the bottle again.

'From the bar,' Jesse said and moved it out of reach.

They watched him go then Luther said, 'Mordecai ain't goin' to be happy about this.'

'Yeah.'

'Have you noticed of late that since Ford arrived in town that our numbers have dwindled some?' Luther pointed out. 'Four men today, two the other day, and Gil. The way things are goin' there'll be none of us left soon. That fool may have run, but he could be right. Ford just may kill us all.'

'It ain't like you to be spooked so easy, Luther,' Jesse commented. 'Is what that fool sayin' gettin' to you?'

Luther tossed back what was left of his glass of rye. 'I ain't spooked, Jesse. Just mighty cautious about dyin'.'

Jesse stoppered the bottle. 'I guess we best go and see Mordecai and see what he wants us to do.'

'He ain't goin' to like it.'

Jesse sighed. 'No. No, he ain't.'

★ ★ ★

'Damn son of a bitch,' Mordecai Wakefield rasped out when he heard that he'd lost another four men. 'I can't believe that one man could cause so much trouble. Where's Talbot?'

'Out in the hall,' Jesse told him.

'Get him.'

Jesse crossed to the door, opened it and mumbled something to Talbot. He entered and Jesse closed the door behind him. Talbot stood next to Luther, and Jesse took station on the other side of him.

Wakefield stared at him for a moment before his face changed to a silent snarl and his right fist lashed out. The wet sound of his punch as it struck Talbot on the jaw filled the room. Talbot staggered but remained upright.

'Damn coward!' Wakefield snarled. 'You run out on your friends. Left them there to die.'

'But . . . but there was nothing I could do, Mordecai,' Talbot stammered as he dabbed at the bloody corner of his mouth.

Wakefield lashed out again. This time, Talbot went down. 'Don't damn well call me Mordecai. How many times do you have to be told?'

There was genuine fear in the man's eyes as he stared up at the vigilante boss.

'Sorry, Judge,' he mumbled through bruised and bloodied lips.

'You will be,' Wakefield said harshly. 'We're goin' back out there to get him. And guess what? You are goin' to be right out front leadin' the way. This time, if you run I'll damn well shoot you in the face.'

14

Eight black-coated riders thundered into the yard of the Galloway homestead with rifles in hand spoiling for a fight. What they found though were the bodies of their brethren that still lay where they had fallen.

All else was quiet. Wakefield gave the order to search the house but they found nothing. The place was deserted.

Wakefield looked about and his horse shifted nervously beneath him at the scent of death that lingered in the mountain air. He frowned. The corral was empty. He signalled to Jesse.

'Go and check out the barn,' Wakefield ordered.

Jesse was gone only a couple of minutes before he returned.

'It's empty,' Jesse explained to him. 'No people, no horses, nothin'.'

Wakefield continued to look around, this time expanding his field of view out further to include the river flats and the low foothills and ridges.

'Luther,' he barked. 'Do a circle of the homestead and see if you can pick up any tracks. I want to know which way they went.'

'Sure boss,' Luther replied as he kneed his bay horse forward.

Steely eyes fixed on Jesse. 'Burn it. The whole lot of it. I want nothin' left standin'. Then we go after them.'

★ ★ ★

A plume of smoke began to billow high into the air as flames took hold, leaving a blackened smudge against the pristine blue of the clear mountain sky. Up on the ridge, in the shade of a large ponderosa, two figures watched as more columns appeared.

'There goes the barn and the other out buildin's,' Leander Galloway said in disgust. 'The blasted animals.'

'I'm sorry about your spread, Galloway,' Ford apologized. 'Once this is over I'll take some time and help you rebuild. Providin' we survive this little encounter.'

'We'll survive it,' Galloway said with grim determination. 'I want to see that bastard hang.'

'If I have my way,' Ford said stoically, 'he won't even set eyes on a rope.'

'I count eight riders,' Galloway pointed out. 'That means there is one or two still in town.'

'Not to worry,' Ford said positively. 'It'll be dark by the time we get there. And even later by the time they work it out.'

Galloway sat there and silently watched on in anger at all that he had built go up in flames.

'Come on,' Ford said as he placed his hand on Galloway's shoulder, 'we got things to do.'

★　★　★

When the shot came it sounded as though the night had been rent asunder. Ford felt the passing of the bullet as it narrowly missed him.

As the sound of the shot rolled along the main street of Stay, Ford heard the grunt of pain as the slug meant for him buried itself into Galloway's middle.

Ford cursed and heeled savagely at the roan's flanks in anticipation of a second shot. The animal lurched forward and the next shot flew through empty space.

The tell-tale muzzle flash gave away the shooter's position at the mouth of an alley between two false-fronted buildings on the left. Ford palmed up a Colt he'd taken from one of the dead vigilantes at the homestead and cut loose.

Ford sent three shots at the hidden shooter, then leaped from the saddle. More shots erupted from the alley and cut the air close to Ford. He returned fire and he heard a curse cut through the darkness.

A man in a long black coat staggered from the alley and brought up his six-gun. He was obviously wounded because his aim was way off. The shots he fired smashed a shop window further along the street.

Ford raised the Colt and squeezed off a shot that smashed into the man's chest and caused him to lurch drunkenly before he fell flat on his face, dead.

Quickly Ford turned and hurried across to where Galloway lay. The homesteader was still alive, but his breathing was ragged. If he didn't get medical attention immediately then he would die.

Ford became vaguely aware of people peeking from doors or windows. Then he thought about the vigilantes. What if there was another one still in town?

A middle-aged man poked his head out a shop door a fraction too long when Ford called to him.

'Hey, you. Get over here.' Ford shouted.

The man hesitated.

'Now, damn it, or this man will die.'

With a few hesitant steps, the man approached.

'We need to get him inside,' Ford told him. 'Your shop will do.'

'I . . . I . . . ahh,' the man stammered.

'Pick him up.'

They struggled with Galloway and managed to get him inside. The dimly-lit store was a drapery and had a high counter upon which the two men placed Galloway.

'Go and get the doc,' Ford ordered.

The man disappeared out the door without a hint of protest. Ford grabbed up some cloth and pressed it against the wound to try and stop some of the bleeding. Galloway gave out a soft moan then went still again. He'd have to come up with a new plan now that Galloway was out of action.

It was almost ten minutes before the man returned with a woman who bore a large bruise on her cheek.

'Where's the doc?' Ford asked.

'After the beating, he received last

night I'm afraid my husband won't be able to come,' Mary Jones said curtly as she leaned over Galloway. 'I'll have to do.'

'No offence, ma'am, but can you fix him?'

'I won't be able to if I stand here talking all night, will I?' she remarked, then sighed. She apologized. 'Sorry, Marshal Ford. It has been a very trying time. I work with my husband at times and he's taught me a thing or two. I think I can fix Leander.'

'I sure do hope so, ma'am,' Ford told her. He turned to the storekeeper. 'Will he be safe here while I'm gone?'

The man looked horrified. 'Gone? Gone where?'

'It's best you don't know,' Ford answered. 'But know this. By the time it's all over, either I'll be dead or The Judge will.'

Ford made for the door but turned back. 'Are there any more vigilantes left in town?'

'No. The others rode out to look for

you,' Mary Jones answered without looking up from ministrations on Galloway.

'That's somethin' I guess,' Ford acknowledged. 'I'll be seein' you.'

'Marshal Ford, be careful,' Mary Jones called after him. 'This town is depending on you.'

★ ★ ★

His first stop was the telegraph office. There was a light on inside and the telegrapher sat reading a battered dime novel by lamplight.

He looked up when Ford entered. His jaw dropped and he blurted out, 'It's . . . it's you.'

Ford ignored him. 'I want you to send two wires. One to Fort Somerset and another to the marshal's office in Helena.'

The marshals there would be able to get word to Bass although he was almost a week away. Fort Somerset, being closer, was where he hoped to get

179

more immediate help from.

'I can't do that,' the skinny man with wire-framed glasses said hurriedly. 'They'll hang me for goin' against The Judge.'

Fear. Everything came down to fear and the people of Stay were the worst he'd seen. But he needed the wires sent. If he failed to inform them of what was happening, and he was killed by Wakefield and his men, then nothing would change.

With a solemn sigh, he took out the Colt, cocked it and placed it on the counter he leaned against.

'Listen . . . ?' Ford paused.

'Stan,' the telegrapher supplied as his eyes fixed nervously on the cocked six-gun.

'Listen, Stan,' Ford said calmly, 'any time now the Judge and what is left of his vigilantes are goin' to come thunderin' back into town and I ain't got time to waste. Now you send them wires. I'll write them so there's no mistake. And I don't need to wait for a reply.'

'But the line to the fort is down.'

'Then do what you can.'

Stan made to protest again but Ford's no-nonsense look stopped him cold and instead he picked up a pencil stub and paper and placed them on the counter.

Hurriedly Ford wrote out what was to be sent then watched as the telegrapher worked his key. After Stan had finished, he left. There was still one more thing to do before he left town.

* * *

Ford worked quickly. He broke into Wakefield's room and moved the sideboard. Behind it was a hole in the wall and inside that were sacks of gold coins. After taking them out, he pushed the sideboard back and opened one of the sacks. He took out a freshly-minted coin and dropped it on the polished surface of the sideboard.

The more thought he gave the situation, the more Ford could only come up with a single course of action. He could run and leave the town at the mercy of Wakefield and his gang of vigilantes or he could fight. There was no real decision to make. He had to stay and fight, but first, he needed to even up the numbers some more.

As Ford looked at the coin he smiled coldly. *That ought to get the son of a bitch's attention,* he thought.

★ ★ ★

The eight men on tired horses finally arrived back in town about two hours before dawn. Out front, Wakefield was not happy. Once more Ford had slipped through their fingers and made them look like fools. One thing was for sure, he'd make him pay. He'd string him up for all of Stay to see.

Wakefield's thoughts were interrupted when he saw the dark lump lying in the street. He frowned. 'What the . . . ?'

All eight men drew their horses to a

182

halt and Jesse climbed down stiffly from the saddle to check the body.

'Is that who I think it is?' Wakefield asked him.

Jesse stood up. 'Yeah, it's Arkansas.'

A surge of anger rippled through Wakefield as he sat and stared at the latest in the body count left behind by Ford. So, he came back to town.

'Jesse, get the boys to get the body off the street, then see if he's still here,' Wakefield ordered.

'You think that Ford did this?'

'Damn right he did it.'

'But why would he come back to town?' Jesse asked.

Wakefield thought for a moment then a thought struck him.

'The blasted telegraph,' Wakefield cursed. 'Check the telegraph office. If he's managed to send word out of here, then we're done. We'll have to move on. Take Luther and check.'

'We all need to get some rest, Judge,' Jesse pointed out.

'We'll rest when I say so,' Wakefield

snapped. 'Now get about it.'

With the others busy, Wakefield went back to his room.

And found the evidence left out for him.

★　★　★

Upon seeing the splintered door jam, a wave of panic washed over Mordecai Wakefield. He drew his six-gun and cocked it. Tentatively he moved into the room, ready for whatever came his way.

As he looked around all seemed in order. Wakefield swept his gaze over everything in the room until he caught a glimpse of the shiny coin on top of the sideboard.

Suddenly his body began to tremble. He took a lurching step forward and halted. Maybe it was a trick of the dim light. Another step and he knew it was no trick. It was a definite taunt in the form of a nice, shiny and new gold coin.

Wakefield's face twisted into a snarl

as he hurried to the sideboard and moved it aside.

The hole was empty. The sacks of coins were gone.

'Damn you to hell!' Wakefield shouted loudly.

There was movement at the door and Jesse and Luther appeared. He turned to face them.

'You were right,' Jesse informed him. 'He sent a wire to Helena, the marshal's office there. But that is a five-day ride. And he wanted to send one to Fort Somerset but the wire is down to there.'

Wakefield digested what Jesse had told him and after some thought, nodded.

'That's good. We'll need the time.'

'Time for what?' Luther asked puzzled.

'Time to get our $50,000 back,' Wakefield said gesturing to the empty hole. 'The son of a bitch cleaned us out.'

15

Mid-morning found Ford squatting down beside a fast-flowing stream with a broad rocky shoreline on both sides, filling his canteen. The foreshore stretched for around thirty feet, all rounded rocks and pebbles until it reached a scree slope that stretched up another forty feet where it stopped at a thick line of conifers.

To his right, the stream turned around a small spit of grassy land and disappeared into the trees. To his left, it was more open but still well wooded. Beyond the trees was a scar-faced cliff topped with yet more trees that seemed to perch precariously on its edge. It was wild, rough country but majestic all in one.

Since he'd left Stay, Ford had pointed the roan north and ridden out beyond the lake and into the surrounding mountains. He was looking for an ideal place to set up and take Wakefield and his bunch without getting himself killed. And as he looked at the rising scree slope beyond the stream, he thought that this might be a good place to start.

Ford walked across to the roan, mounted once more and kneed him forward. Once the horse was in the water, he turned him right and rode downstream until he was around the grassy spit of land. Then he rode out of the stream and up a less severe slope and into the trees.

He circled the horse around until he was abreast of the place where he'd filled the canteen. Then, leaving the roan back a piece and well out of harm's way, Ford dismounted and took the Winchester from the scabbard. He approached where the slope fell away and found cover behind a solid dead fall. Then he sat down to wait.

★ ★ ★

Bass Reeves turned up a queen and placed it on the king. He followed it up with the seven of clubs and could put it nowhere. He softly cursed under his breath as he conceded that the game of solitaire that he was currently playing was not a winner.

'Can I get you anythin', Bass?' Chris the barkeep called out to him from behind his long polished-top bar.

Reeves sighed. 'Maybe a new deck of cards, Chris. These ones don't seem to be favourable at the moment.'

Chris smiled and went back to cleaning the glasses he'd need for when the Crazy Lady Saloon opened later that morning. He looked around the empty bar room and made a mental note of other things that needed to be done.

'Are you leavin' today, Bass?' Chris asked.

Reeves was about to answer the question when the saloon doors opened to admit Lodestone town sheriff, Sandy Johnson, who held up a piece of paper.

Lodestone was a mining town in the Hardrock Mountains and Reeves was there for one reason only. It was close to the Moose River Range.

Johnson hurried over to him and placed the piece of paper on the table in front of him.

'It looks as though you were right, Bass,' he said pointing at the telegram. 'A wire just came in from Helena. It looks like your boy has got himself into some trouble. And that ain't all.'

Reeves picked the paper up and read it slowly. He looked up at Johnson and said questioningly, 'Mordecai Wakefield? I thought he was still in prison.'

'Not hardly, goin' by that,' Johnson stated.

'Damn it,' Reeves swore and tossed the cards he held in his hand on to the table. 'If there is one thing that boy knows how to do, it's get into trouble.'

The chair scraped on the bare floorboards as Reeves stood up.

'What are you goin' to do?' Johnson asked him.

'I'm goin' up there to stomp some snakes,' Reeves informed him.

'That's if there are any left to stomp,' Johnson said. 'I've heard stories about your boy. They say he's a one-man army. A regular lone wolf.'

'You have no idea,' Reeves said grimly. 'Although, of all the marshals I have at my beck and call, he's the one I'd rather have on this job. Them vigilantes have killed two marshals. They won't be killin' any more. Not if Josh can help it. I just hope he leaves enough left over for me.'

'Good luck, Bass,' Johnson said.

'Luck ain't got a damn thing to do with it, Sandy,' Reeves remarked.

* * *

Mordecai Wakefield and his men reached the stream in the middle of the afternoon. Hidden from view, Ford thumbed back the hammer of the Winchester and sighted along the barrel. He moved it until the foresight settled upon a black-coated rider third in line.

Ford breathed out slowly and squeezed the trigger. He felt the rifle slam back against his shoulder and the crack of the shot echoed from the surrounding ridges. Through the gunsmoke, he saw the rider fall from the saddle.

Ford levered another round into the Winchester's breech. He sighted and fired again. A horse buckled under its rider and fell, throwing the vigilante forward on to the rounded rocks of the stream's shoreline.

Below him, the riders began to gather themselves and return fire. While shots cracked overhead, Ford stayed low and pushed himself back away from the deadfall he'd taken shelter behind.

One man was dead, he was certain of that. The other rider, however, would only be stunned unless he'd been unlucky and fallen awkwardly.

But for now, it was time to cut and run. That was until darkness arrived. Then Ford would give them something else to think about.

Wakefield cursed violently when he saw Zeb fall after a bullet tore through his skull. And while he sawed on the horse's reins, trying to wrestle control of the animal back, another shot rang out. This time, Jesse's horse went down with a slug in it, spilling its rider on to the stream's rocky shore.

'Damn it, where the hell is the son of a bitch?' Wakefield shouted as he drew his six-gun.

'Up there in the trees,' Luther called out as he started firing across the stream at the top of the slope. 'Behind that deadfall.'

The rest of the vigilantes opened fire, sending a hailstorm of lead in the direction the shots had come from. They could see great chunks of bark being chewed from the log as the slugs hammered home.

As more gunfire rang out, Wakefield looked down at Jesse who was clambering to his feet.

'Are you alright?' he shouted to be

heard above the din.

With blood running freely from a cut on his forehead, Jesse looked up at Wakefield and nodded.

'Get Zeb's horse, he won't be needin' it,' he ordered. 'And the rest of you, stop firin'! The sonuver's gone! Can't you tell when you're not bein' shot at?'

The gunshots died away and the vigilantes took stock of their situation. One of them was dead and one of the horses had been shot. Which evened out, but Wakefield noted that once more their number had dwindled in strength.

'Talbot?'

The vigilante edged his horse over to beside Wakefield. 'Yeah?'

'I want you to scout ahead,' Wakefield ordered him.

Talbot looked almost mortified. He opened his mouth to speak, but Wakefield stopped him cold.

'Before you say somethin' that is liable to get you shot, think,' the vigilante boss hissed icily. 'Because if you *do* say somethin' I don't like, I'll kill you right here, right now. Your choice. But I sure as hell don't plan on gettin' jumped like that again. Now get the hell out there.'

Wakefield watched him reluctantly ride into the stream. Jesse walked his new mount across the rocky ground and looked up at the vigilante leader.

'You do realize that Luther or even me would have been a better choice to scout, don't you?'

He nodded. 'Yeah. But if Ford does somethin' like that again I'd rather lose that yeller dog than one of you two.'

'What are we goin' to do about Zeb?'

Wakefield looked at the vigilante's body and spat on the rocky ground. 'Leave him there. He ain't goin' to care.'

★　★　★

Not long before sunset when the sky was streaked with orange and red, the seven vigilantes made camp beside a small beaver pond that was surrounded by tall grasses and silver-barked aspen. Back from those were dense copses of conifers, all over a hundred feet in height.

They soon had a small fire going and the dry snap and crackle carried through the still night air. Two men were to remain on watch throughout the night, with a shift change every two hours. They were in wolf country and the valley rang eerily with their lonesome howls. The horses moved about nervously at the picket line, snorting and stomping.

'I wish them wolves would find themselves another place for the night,' Jesse declared. 'The damn things give me the willies.'

'Be thankful it's not somethin' bigger,' Wakefield stated, remembering the grizzly tracks and the half-eaten carcass of the elk they'd come across.

Jesse got his meaning. 'I was tryin' not to think about that. Thanks.'

A heavy silence settled over the

camp, the last thing they needed was a rogue grizzly tearing through their camp.

A vigilante named Link stood up and began to walk away from the fire.

'Where the hell are you goin'?' Wakefield asked him.

'To find a tree to sleep in.'

Wakefield smiled and squirmed down, resting his head on his saddle.

'Wake me when it's my turn for watch,' he told Jesse. 'Or if somethin' happens.'

'Yeah, right,' Jesse said grimly.

But they needn't have worried. At that moment the bear was almost ten miles away. Ford, however, was close. Really close. And he was planning his next move against the vigilantes.

16

Shortly after midnight, Ford decided to make his move. The moon was only a quarter and the stars fought to break through a partial cloud cover.

The night sounds had undergone a significant change. The howls of the wolves had been replaced by the occasional call of night birds and the croak and chirrup of frogs that lived in the beaver pond.

Ford had waited and watched the camp for hours. He'd left the roan far enough away from the camp so it wouldn't be a problem. He'd also left it loose with the reins looped up around the saddle horn just in case any predators came sniffing about. That way the roan could make an easy enough getaway. He left the Winchester in the scabbard and took only the Colt and his knife.

Then Ford circled around the camp to approach from the opposite direction.

He drew the razor-sharp knife and slowly made his way towards the first of the lookouts. The long grass helped his stealthy approach, cushioning his footfalls. Green stalks whispered across his clothes as he pushed through.

The lookout sat with his back against a tall, rough-barked pine, seemingly relaxed with his surroundings. The vigilante stirred and Ford dropped to his right knee and waited for him to settle. The man fidgeted for a brief moment and a small flare erupted in front of his face. This was followed by the distinct smell of tobacco smoke.

Ford shook his head. In a situation such as this, the last thing any lookout should do is give his position away so easily. That was the whole idea of it. To remain unseen.

Ford circled the vigilante and came upon him from the right. The man was totally unaware of the presence of the deputy marshal until it was too late.

There was a sharp burning pain in his throat, which created the instinct to reach up for the source, only to feel the hot gush of blood wash across his hand and down his front.

The vigilante started to topple sideways, but before he'd touched the ground he was already dead and Ford had moved on towards his next victim.

* * *

'Mordecai, wake up,' Jesse whispered urgently into the vigilante leader's ear.

'What?' Wakefield spluttered awake. 'How many times . . . ?'

'Just shut up and listen,' Jesse hissed.

'I guess I'd better,' Wakefield said, his voice taking on a dangerous tone.

He noticed the first golden rays of sunlight edging over the mountain tops as the day started to break. The early morning chill of the mountains pricked his skin and he instantly knew what had Jesse worried. The lookouts hadn't woken them for their turn at watch.

'Link and Talbot are dead,' Jesse informed him. 'Both of them had their throats cut.'

Wakefield went with his first thought and said, 'Indians?'

Jesse shook his head and said, 'Not unless they've taken to wearin' heels.'

'Ford,' Wakefield sighed.

'That would be my guess.'

'Damn that man,' then Wakefield became wary. 'Do you think he's still out there?'

'I don't know.'

'All right, get the rest of them up and we'll have a look around.'

'OK.'

Wakefield watched him hurry off to rouse the others. For the first time, doubt crept into his mind and he wondered just how many of them would be alive by the end of the day.

An hour later Jesse and Luther reported back to Wakefield.

'We found where he left his horse,' Jesse informed him. 'Luther followed his tracks around the camp. He watched us for quite a while before he made his move.'

'Which way did he go?' Wakefield asked.

'That's the strange part,' Jesse said. 'It looks like he's headed back to town.'

'But he's takin' the long way,' Luther put in. 'He's ridin' back the way he came. I could take Wilson's Pass and beat him back to Stay and be there waitin'.'

Wakefield worked it out in his head. Luther was right. Riding hard, he could be back in Stay two hours before Ford reached there. Or if he was lucky, Ford would lay up for the night and not arrive in Stay until the following morning.

'OK, do it,' he agreed. 'Take Purdy with you.'

★　★　★

United States Marshal Bass Reeves rode into Stay mid-afternoon on a horse that couldn't have carried him another mile. He felt much the same way after the ride. He'd pushed hard for most of the night, stopping only for a few hours sleep before continuing.

Riding along the main street he became aware of the attention he was drawing. Citizens stared at him, some pointed.

A small gust of wind funneled between the false-fronts washed over him. It carried with it the stench of rotting flesh. Reeves screwed his nose up at the putrid smell. Although he'd smelled it many times before, it was something he'd never gotten used to.

'So much for the clear mountain air,' he mumbled aloud.

The further his horse ventured into town, the stronger the stink became until he came upon at the source. The open coffin outside the undertaker's business.

Reeves stopped the horse and stared at the abysmal form that had once been Gus Tolliver, complete with badge still pinned to the cadaver's chest. He spat, hawked and spat again as though trying to rid his senses of the disgust he now felt.

'By hell, someone is goin' to pay for this,' Reeves' voice rumbled deep in his throat. 'Some son of a bitch is goin' to pay.'

He guided his horse over to the hitch rail and dismounted. He stomped up the steps and across the boardwalk and tried the doorknob. It showed a little resistance then turned, allowing a furious United States Marshal to enter.

Inside, the light was dim and the smell of embalming fluid hung thickly in the air. The undertaker was a craftsman. Some of his coffins were leaning against a wall. All hand-tooled and some polished with brass handles while others were basic, not much more than a long box.

'Anyone there?' Reeves called out as he approached the counter.

A hawk-faced man with gaunt features and spectacles emerged from the back room wiping his hands on a soiled rag. He looked Bass up and down before saying, 'Not the usual customer I get in here.'

'Is this your joint?' Reeves snapped impatiently.

'It is my place of business, yes,' the man answered.

'Then get out there and get that thing off the board-walk and into the ground,' Reeves ordered. 'Now.'

'I . . . I'm afraid I can't do that sir,' the undertaker stammered. 'Not without permission.'

'Who the hell says so?' Reeves grated.

'The Judge,' the undertaker said hurriedly.

'Well, I'm tellin' you to bury him.'

'Under whose authority?'

Reeves pulled the lapel of his coat aside so the man could see his badge.

'Under my authority. United States Marshal Bass Reeves.'

The man paled. 'Oh Lord.'

'Nope, just me,' Reeves said. 'And while I have you here, you can answer a few questions for me.'

'No! I can't,' the undertaker blurted out.

Reeves took out his six-gun and lay it on the counter. 'Mister, you may be scared of this Judge feller you're talkin' about, but trust me, I'm a damn sight scarier than him. You see, that feller out the front there, in that box, he came here with my son. I received word that my son was in trouble and I'm here to help with said trouble.'

Reeves paused before he spoke again. This time, his voice was full of menace. 'So, I ain't got time to be bandyin' words with you. Especially if it gets my son killed. Let's start again from the beginnin'.'

By the time the undertaker had finished, Reeves knew almost everything there was to know. From the start of all the troubles to the marshals and how they died, and what was happening at that time with the vigilantes hunting Ford in the mountains.

'They found out that he sent word to

the marshals and the army,' the undertaker said. 'But they went after him instead of runnin' themselves. Word has it that he took somethin' from them. When they rode out of here there was only eight of them left. That boy of yours sure has whittled them down some. Maybe it was even luck that they ain't got him yet but you know what they say about luck? It's gotta run out sometime.'

17

There was no point in heading out on a worn out horse, so Reeves found the livery and left it there for the night. After the animal was quartered away he took his saddle-bags, his favoured Winchester '73, and a Loomis coach gun, and found a room at the hotel.

It was small but comfortable, and once he'd gotten squared away, Reeves picked up the Loomis and left the Winchester lying on his bed. He checked the loads out of habit and with that done he snapped it closed and went downstairs.

Reeves walked around town asking questions and getting similar answers. The town was under the heel of the vigilantes and was living in total fear. The Judge hanged anyone he deemed had broken his laws and it didn't matter who they were.

Reeves stopped at the jail and looked about. The gun rack on the wall was full and he found spare ammunition in the cupboard. He stood there thinking before he walked back outside and stopped in the middle of the boardwalk.

Looking about he picked out two men. One a well-dressed middle-aged man and the other a younger-looking cowhand.

'You and you,' he said pointing at them. 'Give me a hand.'

They both hesitated.

Once more, Reeves was forced to open this jacket and show his badge. 'How about now?'

After a quick glance at each other, they followed Reeves inside the law office.

'What are your names?' he asked them.

'Elliott,' said the elder of the two.

'I'm Cully,' the cowhand offered.

'All right, Elliott, you're in charge,' Reeves declared. 'I want you two to get down all the guns from the rack as well as all the ammunition in the cupboard and take it to my room at the hotel.'

'But . . . '

'No buts,' Reeves told Elliott, 'Just go ahead and do it.'

The chain was busted off the rack and the two commenced work ferrying the weapons and ammunition to the hotel. Reeves searched the office for anything else of interest. He searched the cupboard and drawers in the desk. When he opened the last drawer, Reeves looked through it then paused. He stared at the two objects sitting in the bottom then reached down to retrieve them.

He held them up in front of his face to see them more clearly. Both were engraved with the words: UNITED STATES DEPUTY MARSHAL.

He stared at them for a time and was disturbed by a well-dressed man entering the jail. Reeves stuffed the badges into his pocket and stared at the newcomer.

'Hello, I'm . . . '

'What do you want?' Reeves snapped, the anger from his find bubbling to the surface.

The man swallowed and started again. 'I'm Fellows, August Fellows. I used to be mayor of Stay.'

Reeves nodded. 'The name's Bass Reeves, Mr Fellows. What can I do for you?'

'I believe that you are a United States Marshal?'

'I am,' Reeves acknowledged.

'Then I advise you to leave now while you still can,' Fellows urged him.

Reeves sighed. 'I am fully aware of the situation in Stay, Mr Fellows. I ain't goin' anywhere.'

Fellows looked worriedly at Reeves. He ran his eyes over the marshal's greying hair, salt-and-pepper moustache, and his lined face.

'But you are not a young . . . '

A dark cloud came over Reeves' face. 'If you tell me I'm too old to go up against these damned murderin' scum, I'm liable to shoot you. I been takin' down killers like these for most of my damned life. Now where do these rats usually hole up when they're in town?'

'I'll show you,' Fellows answered and started towards the door.

★ ★ ★

The last orange hue from the setting sun reached out across the sky and painted the grey granite faces of the mountains a rich golden colour. Ford caught sight of a large bull elk standing on a ridge looking out over the valley, as he fed another stick into the small fire.

He'd made the decision to lay up for the night because the roan had been pushed hard for the past few days and he needed the rest. He had, however, left the animal saddled just in case.

He would be back in Stay around mid-morning tomorrow and could prepare for the final showdown with Wakefield and his men. And just maybe, he might be able to find some help amongst the townsfolk. Maybe.

211

If he couldn't, he'd have to go it alone. It wouldn't be the first time, but it could be the last.

At least if something did happen to him, Bass would know what was going on. It was just a shame that he wouldn't get back to Bismarck to see Hannah.

Ford lay back with his head on his bedroll and he gazed up at the first twinkle of stars and thought of the slim dark-haired young woman. As he did so, all of the violence and trouble of the past few days caught up with him and he fell into a deep sleep.

★   ★   ★

The Cedar Log had more customers than usual that evening. Perhaps it was because the vigilantes were out of town or maybe because Reeves was in town and dining in the saloon. Whatever the reason, no one really cared.

That was until a rail-thin man with brown hair and brown eyes rushed in and up to the table where Reeves was seated finishing off his meal.

'They're back, Marshal,' he informed Reeves. 'Two of them just rode into town. They're at the jail.'

Reeves nodded slowly, contemplating his next move. He could go out and meet them in the dark but ... No, better to meet them on his terms.

Reeves stood up and walked to the centre of the room and looked about. All eyes had turned towards him and the noise quickly dropped away.

'All right, listen up!' he said loudly. 'Everybody out. The saloon is closin' early tonight.'

'You can't do that,' the barkeep protested.

Reeves' icy stare settled upon him and he said, 'Unless you want a saloon full of people here when the shootin' starts, I suggest you get them all outta here.'

Without having to be told twice, every person in the Cedar Log moved towards the doors, including the whores. Reeves looked about and found the man who'd brought him the warning.

'Hey, you,' he called him over.

The man left the procession and approached the waiting marshal.

'Was there something you wanted?'

Reeves' face became like granite, cold and hard. When he spoke there was flint in his voice. 'You go tell them sons of bitches there's real law in town and he's waitin' for them over in the Cedar Log.'

The man swallowed. 'Word for word?'

'Every damned last one of them.'

'Uh huh.'

Reeves watched him leave and he said softly to himself, 'Time to go to work.'

* * *

'What the hell is goin' on here?' Luther asked as the lamp light started to take effect in the dark room.

The gun rack was empty, the drawers were open in the cupboard and all of the ammunition was gone.

'You don't suppose the townsfolk here have gone and got brave all of a sudden like, do you, Luther?' Purdy asked.

'Surely they wouldn't be that stupid,' Luther stated. 'But somethin' sure happened to the guns and ammunition.'

'Mordecai ain't goin' to like this,' Purdy observed. 'You don't think Ford could have beat us back here do you?'

Luther shook his head. 'Not the way he was goin'.'

The jail door opened and the man Reeves had sent with the message entered hesitantly.

'What happened here?' Luther asked him. 'Tell me now or by God, you'll wish you had.'

The man paled and his fear threatened to get the best of him. He licked his lips nervously before saying. 'He sent me here with a message.'

'Who?' Luther snapped.

'The marshal.'

'Ford?' Purdy asked, shocked at the thought that he had in fact made it

215

back before them.

'No, the other one.'

'He's dead,' Luther reminded him.

The man shook his head. 'No, the new one.'

Taken aback by the news of the new arrival, both men looked at each other in disbelief.

'Who is this new marshal?' Luther asked the man.

'His name is Bass Reeves.'

'Holy cow,' Purdy blurted out. 'It's the old he-bull himself.'

Luther ignored the awe in his voice and asked the man, 'What is the message?'

At first he hesitated, but then it all came out. 'He said to tell them sons of bitches that real law has come to town and is waitin' for you over at the saloon.'

When the man finished he stepped back a pace and waited nervously to see what would happen next. Luther, however, remained calm and turned to Purdy.

'Come on, let's go,' he said to him.

'Go where?' Purdy asked.

'We're goin' to take some of the hide off that he-bull of yours,' Luther explained, 'before he gets more ornery than he already is.'

18

Bass Reeves sat at the table where he waited patiently for the returned vigilantes to show themselves. The empty saloon was deathly quiet, so quiet in fact that the sound of boots on the boardwalk outside seemed uncommonly loud.

Both vigilantes pushed in through the doors and glanced around the empty room. Then one of them spotted Reeves at the far corner table and nudged the other. There was an almost inaudible murmur and the pair started across the room towards him, weaving between the tables and chairs.

They stopped short in front of Reeves and the marshal looked the black-coated, full-bearded men over.

'I take it that you're Bass Reeves?' Luther said as he pointed at the exposed marshal's badge.

Reeves gave them both a disarming smile, but the cold calculating look in his eyes should have been warning enough for the two men.

'Who might you two peckerwoods be?' Reeves asked casually.

'We're the fellers who're goin' to kill you,' Purdy boasted.

'You sound almighty sure of yourself, friend,' Reeves said evenly. 'Now if I was you I wouldn't go countin' all my chickens before they hatched.'

'What he says is true, old man,' Luther snapped.

The smile left Reeves' face and it became like stone. The next words from his mouth dripped with menace.

'Don't let these grey hairs fool you, sonny,' he growled in a low voice. 'I've chewed up and spat out more men who got their ambitions mixed up with their capabilities than I care to remember. Now, if you've a mind to, pull them guns of yours or get the hell to steppin' and don't come back.'

'Heh heh, I told you he was a salty

one, didn't I, Luther?' Purdy cackled.

A silence descended upon the room. An unnerving quiet while the tension between the three men built as they waited to see what each other would do. The catalyst came in the form of the slamming of a door somewhere along the street.

'Let's see how salty,' Luther snarled.

The vigilante's shoulder dipped as he clawed at the butt of his holstered six-gun. The hammer came back as Luther started to lift the gun level and bring it into line with the seated man before him.

Suddenly the scarred tabletop exploded as the Loomis roared from beneath it, sending a deadly hail of small lead balls and razor sharp splinters scything through the air. The effect was devastating, knocking Luther backward, his chest a mass of rags, splinters, and pulped flesh. He crashed against a table and it flipped under his weight, catapulting him to the side where he scattered a chair before he ended up dead on the wooden floor.

Purdy cried out as he caught pellets and splinters in his arm and side. He reeled back as pain shot through his body and he stumbled over the body of Luther. He fell heavily beside the dead vigilante and tried to ignore the burning sensation in his arm and side as he desperately clawed at his six-gun.

Reeves came erect pushing the remains of the partially destroyed table out of the way. He dropped the empty coach gun and palmed up his Colt. The hammer was fully cocked as the six-gun aligned on Purdy.

'Don't do it,' Reeves snapped. 'Not if you want to live.'

Purdy hesitated briefly, but was beyond reasoning and continued his draw. The hammer of Reeves' Colt fell and the gun belched smoke and flame. The slug hit where the gun was aimed and it buried itself into Purdy's gun-arm.

The screech of pain filled the saloon as numbed fingers let go of the six-gun and it fell to the floor.

Reeves moved in and kicked it away from the writhing form.

'Listen up,' he said as he stood over Purdy. 'Where's Ford?'

'Damn it, I'm shot. God it hurts,' Purdy whined.

'I asked you where Ford is?'

'I'm bleedin', Marshal. You . . . aagh.'

Pain shot through Purdy as Reeves toed him in his wounded side.

'Where, damn it?'

When Purdy said nothing Reeves moved to repeat his previous action.

'Wait, I'll tell you,' the wounded man bleated. 'He's on the trail comin' back here. We took a shortcut to get back here ahead of him.'

'How many are doggin' his trail?' Reeves asked.

'Three.'

'What happened to the rest?'

'All dead. That feller is somethin' else when it comes to fightin'.'

'Yeah, I know,' Reeves said absent-mindedly.

'What?'

'Get up? We're goin' across to the jail,' Reeves snapped.

'I can't, I'm wounded,' Purdy complained miserably.

'Either you get up or I'll shoot you there.'

'I told you . . . '

His words were cut short as Reeves grabbed him by the collar and began to drag him towards the doors leaving a trail of blood across the floorboards and the room filled with painful cries.

★ ★ ★

The dry triple-click of the gun hammer going back brought Ford instantly awake and his eyes snapped open. His eyes focused and he found himself staring down the barrel of a cocked six-gun in the early light of dawn. Behind it, the smiling bearded face of Mordecai Wakefield swam into view.

'When you snore, lawman, you sure do make a lot of noise.'

223

'Damn it,' Ford cursed himself for being a fool.

Wakefield motioned with the six-gun he held in his fist. 'Get up.'

Ford climbed to his feet and stood still as Jesse came up behind him and took the Colt from his holster and relieved him of his knife.

'Well Marshal, it looks like you'll hang after all,' Wakefield observed. Suddenly, though, his smile vanished and his voice grew harsh. 'Where's our damned money?'

'I don't have it.'

There was pressure from a gun barrel being forced into his back that was accompanied by an impatient question from Jesse. 'Where is it?'

'Safe.'

'I don't do safe,' Wakefield snapped. 'I do where.'

'If I tell you that, then you'll just kill me here and now,' reasoned Ford.

'How about I plug you now anyway?' Jesse snarled.

'What good would that do?' Ford

remarked. 'If I'm dead, then you'll never find it.'

'All right, knock it off,' Wakefield barked. 'Nobody is shootin' anyone.'

'Sounds good to me,' Ford observed.

'Besides, if we shoot you now, we can't make a spectacle of the hangin' later.'

'You seem to forget that he wired the marshals before he lit out, Mordecai,' Jesse pointed out.

Wakefield glared at him but let it go. 'We'll stick to the original plan about him murderin' Gil.'

Ford snorted. 'Old Bass may be an ornery cuss with a rawhide streak in him as tough as they come, but one thing he ain't is stupid. He'll ride into Stay and stomp on anyone that gets in his way. Includin' you. You know him, Mordecai. After all, he was the one who arrested you all them years ago. And it seems to me that you fellers are a little light on help these days.'

If Ford was after a reaction he got one, for Wakefield lashed out and backhanded him hard. There was a loud, wet smack and instantly the coppery taste of blood filled Ford's mouth.

He spat on the ground and smiled, his teeth stained pink.

'If you want the money, Mordecai, you'll have to take me back to Stay to get it,' Ford advised him. 'If you don't you'll never find it before the marshals ride in.'

'He's right,' Jesse put in. 'We can still kill him after we get the money.'

'Now what sort of arrangement would that be?' Ford asked.

'It's the only one you'll get,' Wakefield answered crossly. 'You make the choice. A bullet in your guts now or one later after we get our money?'

Again Ford smiled, although this one was full of mirth. 'I'll take my chances on after.'

Wakefield nodded. 'I thought you would. Get on your horse.'

Ford walked over to the roan and said softly, 'A little warnin' would have been nice.'

The animal pulled back its lips revealing yellowed teeth.

'It ain't nothin' to smile about,' Ford whispered harshly. 'When this is all done, you and I are goin' to have a serious talk.'

Jesse gave Ford a hard shove, causing him to stagger. Ford turned around and looked at the vigilante and said in a matter-of-fact voice. 'And you I'm goin' to kill.'

19

Reeves decided to wait and see if Ford would turn up before he rode out to look for him. He would give him until after noon and if he failed to appear by then, he would head out. He wasn't keen on the idea of waiting, but his son always had a way of turning up.

Ford was good at what he did, which was the main reason that Reeves had sent him on this current job. Over his years with the marshal's service, Ford had brought down some of the toughest outlaws there were. For Reeves, it was a double-edged sword. To get the worst of them he always relied on Ford, but in doing so it also meant sending his son into harm's way. It was the nature of the beast.

Maybe give it another hour or so, he thought as he took out his pocket watch and looked at the time. Ten o'clock.

He remembered Josh as a kid. Before he'd left him and gone away to the war, he was always getting into something. Hot-tempered even at a young age, and a fighter, trying to take on other kids older and bigger than himself. He guessed it had held him in good stead while he was growing up because of the way he'd turned out.

Reeves looked about the empty jail office.

'Hell,' he said and stood up. The chair he'd been sitting on scraped as it went back. He grabbed his black low-crowned hat from the worn desktop and rammed it on his head. Next, he took the Winchester and the Loomis and started towards the door.

Reeves was about to wrap his hand around the door handle and turn it when the door opened and Fellows almost bowled him over.

'Whoa there, Mayor,' the marshal said as he stepped back a couple of paces. 'Where's the fire?'

'The Judge and the others are back,'

Fellows said urgently. 'They're riding along the street, coming this way.'

Reeves' face became stoic as he nodded. 'Well then, I'd best go and have a talk with him then, don't you think?'

'There's something else,' Fellows added. 'They've got Marshal Ford.'

Reeves paused, thinking.

'What are you going to do?'

'Whatever it takes,' Reeves told him grimly. 'Get everyone off the street. Things are about to get wild.'

After Fellows had disappeared out the door, Reeves checked the loads in his six-gun and double-checked his Winchester. When he walked out of the jail door, he left the Loomis on the desk because the messenger gun would be more of a hindrance than it would be a help for what was about to happen.

* * *

'Somethin's not right, Mordecai,' Jesse opined as he watched the townsfolk of

230

Stay start to disappear from the street.

The two of them rode side-by-side while the final vigilante, Murph, came behind them leading the blue roan with Ford on it, hands tied behind his back.

'Yeah, I think you could be right,' Wakefield admitted as he dropped his hand to rest on the butt of his six-gun. Then he called back over his shoulder. 'Murph, keep an eye out for anythin' that ain't right.'

Ford straightened in his saddle. He'd sensed it too. He rocked fluidly with the motion of the roan as it walked steadily behind the horse in front of it. Then someone out front near the jail moved into the street. Ford smiled. Now the vigilantes were about to get a taste of real justice.

'Brace yourself, Mordecai,' he jibed, 'you're about to have a real bad day.'

'Murph, keep your gun on him. If he gives you any trouble, kill him.'

The horses eased to a stop in loose formation on the street and from Reeves' position he had a clear line of sight on all of them. He stood there with the Winchester levelled from the hip and fully cocked.

'I see you got my boy there, Mordecai,' Reeves observed. The fact that there was a gun pointed at Ford didn't go unnoticed. 'Looks to be a might tied up, though. He been givin' you some trouble?'

'He took some money that don't belong to him, Bass,' Wakefield explained, rubbing at his beard. 'That and killed some of my men.'

Reeves looked across at Ford. 'Is that true, Josh?'

'You could say that.'

'Did they deserve it?'

'Every last one of them.'

Reeves shifted his gaze back to Wakefield. 'It might be best if you untie him and turn him over to me, Mordecai.'

'Not until I get my money, Bass,' Wakefield insisted. 'And then he's goin' to hang for murder.'

A period of silence ensued as they

sized each other up, although Wakefield's posture in the saddle told Reeves that the man was confident that the outnumbered marshal wasn't in a position to try anything.

'I almost forgot, Mordecai,' Reeves remembered, 'I met a couple of your men last night. They came to see me and we had ourselves a little chat. By the time we finished, we'd reached an understandin'.'

A look of concern was hidden by Wakefield's beard. 'Where are they?'

'I got one feller in jail.'

'And the other?' Jesse asked.

'He's dead.'

Jesse cursed softly. 'Damn it, Mordecai, let's just kill him and be done with it.'

But there was uncertainty in Wakefield's eyes. The fact that Reeves was willing to brace all three of them, even though they had Ford, was disconcerting.

Reeves' eyes darted to Ford who noticed the look and returned it with an almost imperceptible nod. Then Reeves turned his attention back to Wakefield.

The uncertainty was still there. So was the opportunity.

The Winchester moved marginally and the hammer dropped. The .45-.70 slug smashed into Murph's head just above his right eye and killed the vigilante instantly. When he toppled from his horse, Ford launched himself sideways from the back of the roan and crashed heavily on to the street.

Reeves switched his aim and began to fire as quickly as he could, sending bullets into the ground at the horses' hoofs that Wakefield and Jesse rode. The animals panicked and pranced about which made it near impossible for them to shoot accurately.

'Get up and move, Josh,' Reeves shouted. 'Come this way.'

Ford scrambled to his feet and ran towards Reeves who was backing slowly towards the cover of a long water trough.

Sawing on his mount's reins, Wakefield tried hard to bring it under control. There was no hope of him or Jesse returning fire with their horses doing what they were so he shouted to the struggling man. 'Get off the horse. It's the only way.'

Both men leaped from their saddles and ran for cover on the other side of the street. Up on the boardwalk, outside the dry goods store, were some barrels and crates that would offer something solid to hide behind and they both took advantage. They ducked in behind them and opened up with their six-guns.

Reeves and Ford meantime had reached the cover of the water trough and laid down behind it. Reeves untied the rope around Ford's wrists while slugs began to hammer into the wood of the trough or ricochet over their heads.

'What the hell are you doin' here?' Ford asked Reeves as he threw the rope away.

'You're welcome,' Reeves answered.

A bullet passed close overhead and

Ford ducked lower.

'Here,' Reeves said, offering Ford his Colt.

'Did your horse have wings or somethin'?' Ford persisted as he started to return fire at the shooters across the street.

Reeves finished thumbing fresh rounds into the Winchester's loading gate and said, 'I was over in Lodestone. I had me a feelin' that you'd need some help so I camped out there. Looks like I was right.'

Reeves fired two shots at the vigilantes and splinters flew from the crate that Jesse was hiding behind. Return gunfire smashed the window of the sheriff's office and another slug chewed wood chips from a hitch-rail nearby.

Ford fired the last two rounds in the Colt's cylinder. 'I need some more cartridges.'

Reeves sighed at the inconvenience and unbuckled his gun belt. 'Take it. I got rifle shells in my pocket.'

Ford hurriedly strapped it on and

reloaded while Reeves kept up the fire.

'We ain't doin' much good like this, Josh,' he grumbled. 'We could lay here all day and throw shots at each other and get nowhere.'

Ford nodded. 'Cover me while I try to outflank them.'

'Keep your head down.'

Ford was about to break cover when Wakefield and Jesse beat him to it. They parted ways, each running in separate directions along the boardwalk.

'They're runnin', Bass.'

'Which one do you want, Josh?'

'You take Mordecai,' Josh shouted as he stood up. 'I made that other feller a promise.'

'Don't go gettin' yourself shot,' Reeves called after him as he started to chase after Jesse.

'They already shot me once,' he called back. 'I don't plan on lettin' them do it a second time.'

Reeves watched as Ford disappeared around the corner of the dry goods store in pursuit of the fleeing Jesse and turned his gaze to the retreating Mordecai Wakefield.

'Damn it,' he cursed and broke into a jog. 'I'm gettin' too old to be chasin' people.'

Wakefield detoured off the boardwalk and disappeared into the Pink Palace. Reeves followed him inside and stopped in the foyer. He could hear the thump of footsteps coming from the first-floor hallway followed by the slamming of a door.

Behind the desk was a well-dressed, rounded woman with half a yard of make-up on her face. Her dark hair was bundled atop her head.

'How many rooms you got upstairs?' Reeves asked.

'Eight.'

'How many girls?'

'One in each.'

'Customers?'

The woman shook her head.

Reeves nodded and turned away. He crossed to the stairs, gripped the hand-carved balustrade and began to climb. When he reached the top, he eased his head around the corner of the hallway to ensure that it was empty. It was a semi-dark recess without the wall lamps being lit, made even more so by the dark timber wall panels.

Reeves stepped out into the open and took slow steps until he came level with the first door. He stopped and listened carefully. There was movement in the room. He thought about kicking the door but hesitated and moved on to the next.

It was the same. Reeves repeated his actions until he'd taken in all of the doors and when he'd finished he turned to face along the hallway. He walked silently back along the hall until he stood outside of room four. He paused for a brief moment then stepped forward. Beneath his boot a floorboard creaked and Reeves stopped cold.

A slug from inside the room exploded through the thin door just missing Reeves' head by inches. Sharp splinters peppered his face, drawing blood from his cheek and chin. Another shot came and more splinters flew as Reeves reeled back away from the door.

He thought about returning fire through the door like Wakefield, but couldn't be sure whether there was a working girl in there with him.

'Think, damn it,' Reeves mumbled. Then an idea came to him.

Moving to the adjacent door, Reeves tried the handle but found it locked. He drew back his right leg, kicked hard and the door crashed back.

From inside the room next door, more gunfire erupted and bullets punched through the paper-thin walls. On the floor, Reeves saw a working girl in a nightgown take cover with her hands over her head.

'Stay down,' he ordered her.

Abruptly the gunfire stopped and Reeves realized that Wakefield had emptied his six-gun and was busy reloading. Forgetting his plan, he hurried back out into the hall and kicked the door in on the room where

Wakefield was holed up.

The man was standing in the middle of the room fumbling with his six-gun. His jaw dropped when the door burst open to reveal Reeves standing there holding the Winchester on him. Wakefield smiled wanly and said, 'I give up.'

'I'm sure you do,' Reeves snapped and squeezed the trigger.

The first slug hit Wakefield high in the chest leaving a bloody hole on impact. Reeves levered and fired three more times and the vigilante boss did a macabre dance of death before he finally succumbed and fell to the floor.

'You'll be killin' no more marshals, you son of a bitch,' Reeves cursed the dead man.

There was movement to the left of the room and he swung the rifle about to cover the new threat. He needn't have bothered. On the floor was the working girl he'd been worried about, huddled up in a ball, trembling.

'Ma'am?' Reeves said softly. 'Ma'am, look at me.'

Hesitantly, she removed her shaking hands from the top of her head and looked up at Reeves.

'It's OK, ma'am,' he assured her. 'It's all over.'

20

Jesse snapped off a couple of shots at Ford which ricocheted off an awning post, chewing splinters from the upright before they whined harmlessly away.

Ford fired two of his own after the fleeing man, only to see no effect.

He had followed Jesse down the alley beside the dry goods store and out the back where the vigilante had suddenly turned to face him and started firing again. Ford was forced to dive behind a wood pile and wait until he'd finished shooting. Slugs whistled close, chewing off chunks from the short logs.

After a brief exchange, Jesse was up and moving again. He ran down another alley and back out to the main street. Ford followed him and was lucky not to be shot through his carelessness. When he was halfway along the alley, Jesse appeared from around the corner and opened fire.

Ford dived to the hard-packed earth and snapped off a shot that clipped Jesse in the arm as he ducked back. Ford heard the cry of alarm escape the vigilante's lips before he heard the clomp of boots retreating on the boardwalk as he ran away.

Picking himself up, Ford hurried to the alley mouth and peered around the corner to see the fleeing back of Jesse further along.

Walking steadily along the boardwalk, Ford followed close enough to keep the man in sight. Then something caught his eye and he looked down. Ford had been right. He'd hit Jesse and the splashes of blood on the planks confirmed it.

He looked up again and saw Jesse cross the street and disappear into the livery stable. It appeared that his left arm dangled limply at his side.

Immediately Ford crossed the street and slipped down an alley between the bank and the lands office. As he did so, he found two townsfolk hiding behind a pile of discarded junk. They sprung up from behind it, hands at shoulder height and one of them cried out, 'Don't shoot!'

'Get outta here and go home,' Ford ordered them and kept going, cursing them under his breath.

When he exited the alley, he could see the rail corral out the back of the livery. Inside it were two horses. Ford emptied the chambers of the Colt and thumbed in all fresh loads.

He edged his way along the back of the buildings until he reached the livery. The double back doors were open and Ford glanced around the corner to see Jesse, with his back turned, struggling one-handed with a saddle, trying to get it on a horse that moved sideways with each attempt. Ford moved out into the open.

'Give it up,' he said to the struggling vigilante. 'It's over.'

Jesse froze and dropped the saddle. He turned slowly and faced Ford who could see the blood-slicked left sleeve on the shirt.

Jesse lifted his head defiantly. 'What now?'

'That's up to you,' Ford explained. 'You can come along peaceful like and get the rope. After a fair trial, that is.'

'Or?'

'Or you can do somethin' stupid and I'll kill you right here, right now. Your choice.'

'There is a third choice,' Jesse pointed out.

'Which is?'

'I kill you and ride out of here.'

Ford smiled. 'Ain't goin' to happen.'

'How about we find out,' Jesse said, trying to sound confident. He knew deep down he'd never beat Ford, but he had nothing left to lose. He was dead either way.

'OK,' Ford approved, slipping Reeves' Colt back into its holster. 'Any time you're ready.'

Jesse licked his lips nervously and

stared into Ford's eyes. 'I ain't goin' to hang.'

'Then you can die here,' Ford said harshly and drew.

Jesse didn't even try to clear leather. He was a beaten man and he knew it. He'd resigned himself to die this way rather than the long walk up the gallows steps.

Ford didn't have to shoot him six times. Once did the job. The first slug punched his ticket right between his eyes. It wasn't enough. Not for Ford. There had been too many deaths because of these men, some of whom had been his friends. The last five bullets were for them.

'Josh? Are you OK?' Reeves called from outside the front entrance.

Ford was replacing the empty cartridges when Reeves called him. 'Yeah, in here.'

Reeves entered the livery and Ford turned to face him. 'Wakefield?'

'Dead.'

'Good.'

'I see your feller ain't causin' any more problems.'

They were both silent for a moment when Reeves broke it by asking, 'Where did you hide the money?'

'The best place for it.'

'Huh?'

'It's in the bank,' Ford explained.

Reeves shook his head in bewilderment. 'Son of a . . . '

'I woke the bank manager up before I left town. He's got it in his safe. I figured that was as good a place as any. The vigilantes were stealin' from the shopkeepers, but for some reason, they were leavin' the bank alone.'

Ford started to walk off when Reeves asked, 'Where are you goin'?'

'I got some people to check up on.'

★ ★ ★

Galloway looked gaunt and pale but at least he was still alive. And by all reports was likely to stay that way. His wife had come to town on hearing the

248

news and remained by his bedside.

'You look like you should be dead,' Ford said with a smile, glad to see him still alive.

'I see you're still breathin' too,' Galloway said weakly.

'I assume that by you standing here, Marshal, that it is over. Is it true?' Nora asked.

'Yes, ma'am, the vigilantes are no more,' Ford confirmed.

'Thank God,' Mary Jones sighed from where she stood next to Galloway's bed.

'You did a good job, ma'am,' Ford congratulated her. 'How is your husband?'

'He's fine,' Mary answered. 'Although he'll still be laid up a while.'

Reeves entered the room and Nora Galloway focused on him. 'Here is another man we have to thank for saving our town.'

'I didn't do much, ma'am,' Reeves told her. 'Josh here did all the hard liftin'.'

'Still, without your help we . . . '

Reeves put up a hand to halt her.

'Oh for cryin' out loud, old man,' Ford snapped. 'Will you just shut up and accept what you're bein' told.'

Reeves' gaze hardened as he stared at Ford.

'Don't take that tone with me, boy,' Reeves admonished.

Ford shook his head. 'Anyway, I'm off.'

He turned to leave when Reeves called after him. 'Hold hard there, Josh. Where do you think you're goin'?'

Without looking back, Ford said loudly, 'Bismarck. But first I have somethin' else to do.'

'What?'

'Help rebuild a homestead.'

'We still got stuff to do here,' Reeves shouted after him but Ford ignored him and kept going. 'What about the prisoner?'

'That's a good man you have there, Marshal,' Nora Galloway observed.

'Yes, ma'am, he is that,' Reeves

allowed. 'Among other things.'

'Have you known him long?'

Reeves nodded. 'Long enough, ma'am. He's my son.'

We do hope that you have enjoyed reading this large print book.

Did you know that all of our titles are available for purchase?

We publish a wide range of high quality large print books including:
Romances, Mysteries, Classics
General Fiction
Non Fiction and Westerns

Special interest titles available in large print are:
The Little Oxford Dictionary
Music Book, Song Book
Hymn Book, Service Book

Also available from us courtesy of Oxford University Press:
Young Readers' Dictionary
(large print edition)
Young Readers' Thesaurus
(large print edition)

For further information or a free brochure, please contact us at:
Ulverscroft Large Print Books Ltd.,
The Green, Bradgate Road, Anstey,
Leicester, LE7 7FU, England.
Tel: (00 44) 0116 236 4325
Fax: (00 44) 0116 234 0205

LEGACY OF A GUNFIGHTER

Terry James

Following his release from prison, all gunfighter Luke Nicholls wants is revenge against William Grant, the man who almost killed him. Unfortunately, when the two meet, things don't go as planned. Struck down by a mysterious malady, his confidence is shaken. More complications arise when a woman out to avenge the murder of her husband tries to enlist his help. He refuses, determined not to lose sight of his own ambition — but Grant has other ideas. Dragged into a fight for survival, the odds are suddenly stacked even higher against Luke . . .

Other titles in the
Linford Western Library

IRON EYES THE SPECTRE

Rory Black

Having delivered the body of wanted
outlaw Mason Holt to the sheriff at
Diablo Creek, infamous bounty hunter
Iron Eyes collapses, badly wounded,
and his would-be sweetheart Squir-
rel Sally desperately tries to find a
doctor. However, Sally is unaware
she is heading into a perilous uncharted
desert where a mysterious tribe of
Indians lives. Then when Holt's older
brothers discover their sibling is dead,
they vow revenge and set out after
the man who killed him. Soon both
outlaws and Indians realize how dangerous Iron Eyes is . . .

THE GUNMAN AND THE ANGEL

George Snyder

Beautiful Mandy Lee enjoys an elegant and genteel life in North Carolina, but hides an unconventional past. Raised by gunfighter Dan Quint, Mandy is quick on the draw and harbours a burning need for revenge against Monte Steep, the man who murdered her family. And when she learns that Dan, who has his own reasons for hunting Steep, has finally tracked him down, she has to decide whether to forego her life of luxury and her rich fiancé to rejoin him on his quest for vengeance.

GUNPOWDER EMPIRE

Matt Cole

When Luke Bragg comes to Preston Gulch to claim the sheep ranch his uncle left for him, he soon finds himself in the middle of a range war with the valley's two biggest cattle ranchers. This clash of interests only escalates, and the cattlemen claim that Bragg's sheep are killing the grass by nibbling it too close and trampling the roots. Then when the daughter of another rancher comes to town after the murder of her father, the truth about the killing sends the valley into chaos . . .